Fire in the Belly

Charles E. Jambor

PREFACE

Fire In the belly... well, just think about this. Hold on for a few seconds and remember what went through your mind when you read this: fire in the belly. Do you know anyone who really had a fire in their belly? No? But to write a book, you must have a burning desire in your gut, a fire to write. I begin with this melodramatic statement because it deals with fire, and it has action in it. At the end, I escape the fire.

The image of a male on the cover is shown at the exact moment of his demise. He has been blown up. You need to see the image here because you want to remember it forever. My book you'll forget in a couple of weeks or in a year. Maybe you'll never forget the book because of the image on the cover.

Kaput, by the way, means dead in the Russian language.

Now, that didn't take very long, going from the beginning to the end of the book in less than thirty seconds.

So, I'll explain. I do not die in a fire, but someone will. You'll be safe while I sort this calamity out. Your guttural feeling of death in a fire will go away. I am not saying it will stay away forever, but it will go away for the time being.

I must also bring your attention to a scientific phenomenon which is advancing upon us so fast that unless you perished in a fire or war, you'll have to put up with yourself thirty or forty years longer.

Aside from creating smarter robots, we first should find out what our extraterrestrial visitors are up to. Because in thirty or forty years, due to alien interference, we could all be gone. It could happen just like it happened many times before. They are watching us now and it is plain to see we are getting close to their level of knowledge. And, when we're almost there… they'll cancel us.

But if there are no humans around – no one will know we're gone. For the time being, I'll deal with the circumstances as they arrive.

Previously in my life, I escaped from my own country, but it is different this time. I'm shackled and restrained somewhere. I don't even know where.

I remember the plane landing at the Jose Marti airport in Havana to pick up passengers, but then several G2 personnel came on board (the State Intelligence Agency of the Government of Cuba) and arrested me, not Olly. They must have been after me. Did they want to get even with me for some of my old sins?

I might as well introduce myself. I am Charles, 75% Hungarian and 25% Jamaican, but no one questions my pedigree.

In this story, I am the protagonist who had an unconventional childhood. One day I started watching WWII on the Smithsonian channel and began having recurring nightmares about that war.

Recently my former employer at a private company – Agency Intel (AI) passed away and everyone was let go. The employer's family sold this fast moving, and at most times, intense business to a man named Olly.

At Agency Intel, I used to be an engineer and a computer programmer.

YOU NEED TO KNOW:

Planet E28 and E26 are only two of the cluster of planets in our Solar System. 28 means the number of light years it takes to travel there; 26 is figured the same way. Even though E26 seems to be a lesser distance, the former is more favorable in the writer's mind. You'll see why.

28 in light years in the universe equals 28 hours in space.

CONTENTS

CHAPTER ONE
THE DREAM

I'm tired this morning. Tired? Why do I feel tired? I am just a child. Children are not supposed to feel tired when they wake up in the morning. There is no shelling out there, so Uncle Paul and I have a chance to bury the dead all day. Uncle Paul instructs me to dig a hole a foot deep, pull the corpse in it and cover it in the soil. I am supposed to go through the corps' pockets and if I find any ID, put it under a stone on the top of the grave. On the spade handle, Paul shows me how much a foot is. I am a little apprehensive because sometimes I don't know if the soldier is dead or just injured. He tells me not to worry; they are all dead. Uncle tells me if the corpse is decapitated, make an effort to find the head. He cautions me about humps on the ground as they could be land mines. He tells me and proceeds to show me how to locate mines and how to defuse them. Uncle Paul is seven years older than myself. I am nine years old. I'm learning about grenades and probably know more about them by now than the guy who invented them. I know all about ammunition too, land mines, rockets and katyushas – multiple rocket launcher. There are about ten of them on our hill, with as many as 48 tubes each. We saw them blazing the other night, raining hell on the Germans, who were about ten kilometers down in the valley. The Germans call them "Screaming Mimmies." Katyusha, by the way, is a pretty Russian girl who pines for her boyfriend, who is away in the front. I don't know if he ever comes back to her, but I really hope he does. There is a lovely song about this girl, Katyusha. A young Russian soldier named Roman sang the song for me and played the tune on a harmonica. I liked the song so much, I asked him to repeat it time after time. When he finished singing, he showed me how to play the harmonica myself. I picked it up right away. In fact, played the music so well he gave me the harmonica to keep. I asked him why he would want to do that. He said he'll be killed in the battle anyways.

Every night, I try to get rid of this recurring dream. I'm sitting in a spaceship way above the earth and through a window watching the war. The explosions appear to be magical. Each one is a 'starburst' and the rockets are like sparklers. Down below, the tracer bullets are crisscrossing and appear to be swimming in slow motion, not in a straight line but in irregular curves. I see the Germans firing back at our hill. I see really big explosions. We must be under German occupation now or just taken over by the Russians. I dream as if this is happening in a theatre. My grandparents, Paul and I are in a cave; a wine cellar dug in the side of a hill. Despite constant explosions, there's nothing falling from the ceiling. Had it caved in, we would have all been killed. I envision this happening and search for a solution to get out of this dream – a nightmare, but I can't. Maybe tomorrow. I always hope that tomorrow I'll escape from this recurring dream. Paul is up now and so are my grandparents. Paul sticks his nose out to check whether we are going to be dealing with Russians or Germans. *"Ruskies"* Paul hollers back assuredly as he walks to the front of the wine cellar. *"The barn's okay, Betsy's alive,"* he yells, and we jubilate. The Ruskies chasing the Germans are moving their equipment down into the valley. We'll have breakfast in the house, Paul declares happily. It is nine or ten o'clock. I don't yet have a watch, but Paul says it's nine thirty. I'm going to find a watch on a dead soldier one day like Paul did a week ago. I found lots of arms, legs and bodies all mangled up, but no watch. He found a fine time piece, an Omega, on a German corpse. Russian soldiers don't usually have watches, most of them come from poor peasant families. I continue my dream and see Grandma milking Betsy and boiling some milk. We break up some stale bread and put it into the milk. Paul swallows a spoonful of it

2

and inhales deeply and he looks down at his pant legs. They are covered in dried blood, maybe brains too. He doesn't care. There will be more blood and mud on them today. I too have long pants on, but mine are not bloody because I have to drag the corpses. He picks them up. There's no shelling now. The Ruskies must have won. I don't see any soldiers close by either. I just see them as they are moving down the hill with their equipment. I hope nobody died, especially Roman, who gave me the harmonica. I don't want to see a hill full of dead Ruskies. Paul tells me, sometimes the Germans use shells filled with mustard gas. We'd know if they used it last night because we would smell it in the air, and we would be dead soon after. Everyone would die. My mother said Paul was a little slow, but I really don't know what she means. I know he doesn't move too fast on his feet, but I don't think that's what my mother thinks. As we prepare to do our daily routine, we walk around the hundred-year-old earthen house with its canted roof. Paul says we might have an easy day today. The Ruskies bury their own dead. There is no damage to the house, but the vineyard is pockmarked by explosions. "Ay-yay, ay-yay" Paul cries, we've lost a lot of grapevines. Ay-yay, ay-yay, we will re-plant though, there's time," he says. "When the war is over, we'll start new cuttings from vines. It takes about three weeks for roots to sprout," Paul says. He describes the grape harvest and how grandpa uses a press to make wine and how he candles the barrels to get them ready. I ask Paul what candling means. "Grandpa lights a candle and lowers it with a wire into a barrel to see if it is clean enough, he explains.

CHAPTER TWO
REALITY

I open my eyes, but they hurt as if they had been shut or taped shut. I'm in pain, great anguish and I hear screams in the breaking daylight. My eyelids are heavy, but I must see. I am dizzy, but I force myself to squint repeatedly. I'm trying to figure out where I am.

I want to raise my right hand to help my eyelids, but I can only lift it about six inches. My hands are shackled to a chain, and so are my feet. It is raining. Through a narrow gap of dirt and rainwater, I am looking at a dystopian place that could easily be called the abyss of hell. I have come close to hell a few times in my life, and I have almost died on several occasions. Did I have a near death experience? Or an out-of-body event? The state I'm in now... could be the final episode. Everything around me is blackened and scorched. I must be at my grandpa's farm because his field looks just as black as this one. The whole acre and half of wheat got on fire, right before harvest. This could have happened by accident; he was a pipe smoker. On the other hand, he might have sat on the field on fire out of revenge.

He could have been angry at the communist secret police for confiscating the family's only bag of flour just before Christmas. The wind could have carried the burning cinders to the next three farms and burned them down too. They surmised it had to be the wind. A confiscated bag of flour here a bag or two there. The communists had to eat bread too.

There is fire ahead of me. Is it a burning body I'm looking at? Losing your life in a fire has got to be the most frightful and painful experience. Especially if you are tied up and can't escape.

How did I get here and how long have I been here? What time is it now? My wristwatch is gone. Should I be glad because I've survived something?

How come I am sitting on stone, or a cinder block or a rock and my back is against a flat bar? Have I been drugged?

Do I still have all my organs? My liver, kidneys, lungs? I must have my heart, but it feels heavy and is racing. I am overwhelmed with these thoughts, and I hurt everywhere.

With a slit for my eyes, I see an intensely burning body that too is or had been sitting on something black, but had fallen forwards and is lying half way on its side. It had to have been a male, my tormenter? This was a man, because I can see the bottom of his left shoe. He is on higher ground. He had to be a big man because the shoe was at least a size fourteen. My eyes are swollen. Looking through them is like staring through tall grass, or am I looking through my upside-down eyelashes? I have to blink repeatedly to restore my vision. From here, as I can see, the fire is in his belly but that can't be. The fire must be away from him because it is burning so fiercely. The flame is about twenty feet high or higher. It hurts to look up. The fire seems to be coming from the same level as his stomach is. I need to swallow; is it soot I'm swallowing? It tastes bitter. I need water to wash it down, but I don't have any. Maybe I'm just swallowing the smoke coming from the burning body…

There is no head on the corpse or if there is, I can't see it. Someone's husband, someone's son, a warehouse employee, delivery person, an office worker, caught in a pipeline explosion of gas or oil? In the haze, I can only see a thin layer of oil on a patch of water and blackened earth that surrounds the burning corpse. The oil is not burning. Further out there are some charred, jagged tree stumps, but no large debris. This is the most disturbing and macabre thing I've ever seen. I am a ball of nerves; I must relax, I tell myself over and over and over.

I could have been transported here or I may have walked here by myself when I was half conscious, crazy, or mindless. It's not likely since I'm strapped to this stone that's shaped like a chair or feels like a chair with a flat bar in the back and maybe glued to it too? Somebody must have put me here.

That's it. Someone drugged me and manacled me when I was unconscious. Is the world gone and I am the only survivor? If there was a war, did the Ruskis win the war? Did some aliens do this to me? Was it an atomic disaster and if it was, I don't want to live anyways? My skin should be peeling off. Maybe it is. I can't touch any of my skin.

What happened to me? I can't sit here doing nothing. Relax, relax, I'm telling myself. The body ahead of me keeps right on burning in the same area, except perhaps more fiercely. Is there going to be an explosion? Should I be running away? I am trying to stand up. I can't. I seem to be stuck to this blackened rock. How am I going to stand up? I think undoing my pants might help. The belt around my waist feels like it is made of steel, like a flat spring in an old wind-up clock, only wider. But it has holes in it for a buckle or pin it can't be steel.

Why would my belt be made of spring steel? I was dressing up in the morning and I used the third hole in my belt because I lost four pounds. I used the second hole before. There is no shelling, and the burning body has no smell. There is usually a bad odor when a human body burns. How far is that body from here – maybe a hundred feet, one-twenty-five?

As I open my eyes a little more, I can see the smoke from the corpse is rising straight up and seems to culminate in a tiny mushroom puff. Is this a nuclear fire? I don't know. Strangely, I am alive. I try and try but I can't see past the tree stumps sticking up from the distant terrain. And I don't see a lake, a river or a creek and there is no sun. May be its cloudy. Or the air is full of smoke. I can see myself. I'm alive. How can I find out if I am

6

still alive? I can see the burning body, but why is it not being consumed by the flames? I look at the shoe again. It is made of leather, sewn, and the sole is attached with wooden tacks. My eyesight is coming back slowly.

They used to make shoes like that in Europe. Am I in Europe? Where is the other leg of this man? Tucked under his body? Without undoing my pants, I am trying to wiggle out of them. I can't. The belt is too tight, and I can't move sideways either. I am 160 pounds now, not much less than I used to be. Maybe I could have gotten the belt off if I had left it in the second hole. Yesterday, yesterday…? I tightened my belt yesterday. No, it couldn't have been yesterday because I was dressed up in a suit and tie and weighed myself because the scale was right there. I was surprised. I am usually heavier. I took a suit out of my closet. It hasn't been worn in a while. It is light brown and has thin dark vertical pinstripes. My shirt is purple, and I put on a tie with inch wide horizontal stripes of gold, green, navy and burgundy, very striking. I remember smirking and asking myself was I going to a fashion show. I was going to meet someone important. I had been talking to this man who sounded like he was the proprietor of some kind of business, or a factory and he wasn't the guy burning here. He was shorter, about my height. How do I know this? I must have been talking to this employer in person, but where? He was impressed with my innovative programming style. How did he know my style? Where were we… or where was I?

He knew I was an engineer, used to write programs and had designed software for different systems. I was going to be his chief programmer. His name is Olly. He said he was the world's largest firearms and ammunition manufacturer. Firearms? Rather primitive. Now-a-days everything is done by 'PIN's' (Plasma Ionizing Nihilation) drones.

He impressed me with the knowledge of the materials his plant used; steel rods and brass rods, barrels of special gunpowder and chemicals that came in boxes and barrels. The raw materials were unloaded at one end of the plant and at the other end the explosives, guns and ammunitions were boxed and put on pallets and into shipping containers and carted away on multiple RVs (remote vehicles).

We are sitting at a table, and he is talking; "the manufacturing in the factory is completely automated, no employees to worry about," he chuckles. I look attentive and laugh aloud because I want him to see I'm paying attention. The money he offered me was really good, and the bonuses were out of this world. All expenses paid, travel… but, travel to where?

I can picture automated machines working, making guns, ammunitions, grenades for people to kill people. If he meant humans, he must have been talking about people in uprisings, tribal wars, like in Afghanistan, Iran, Iraq… maybe I'm being tortured in one of those countries now. Or maybe in the Philippines, Jamaica, or Ukraine. Maybe our own robots have risen up against us and wiped everybody out. Or maybe our robots were fighting invading robots from other planets. Nothing is left but small arms again. Back to the beginning, back to the horse and buggy days. Impossible!

Where was the meeting at? Where did I meet Olly? He wasn't Muslim. He was Caucasian though, maybe Turkish, Dutch? He was about five feet ten inches tall. He had a slight accent, perhaps Russian? But it wasn't a Russian accent, I would have recognized that because I speak Russian. So, was he Ukrainian or German? He wasn't Hungarian. I would have known if he was. Holy moly! Maybe it is him burning there?

No way! The guy burning seems bigger but I can't see his head; must be under his body. He certainly doesn't appear to be wealthy. Nobody I know would wear shoes that were hand made. He's got to be from a European country. Is he from Iran, Iraq, India, Pakistan, or Afghanistan? My God, what happened?

Is his head around here somewhere? Paul always told me to look for the head. I am trying to move my head again, but my neck is stiff, and it hurts when I attempt to tilt it in any direction. I try to rotate my whole body, but there's no way I can move either my lower extremities or the upper in any direction any more than twenty degrees. What in the hell happened to me? I've got to figure this out. I can see if I blink often enough. I can roll my eyes, although it feels as if I have sand in them. I am in a situation I've never been before. Panic! I must relax. I can't panic. My heart is pounding. I can feel it. Am I in a desert? In Death Valley, Mojave Desert, Area 51, Las Vegas, ha-ha-ha, Sahara? I can wiggle my nose. I can speak, or can I?

"Hello, hello," I can shout. Someone is answering or hollering something in a fading voice. Desperate cries coming from the rear, I don't understand the words. Could it be a call for help? I don't see anyone ahead of me. But, but what is that sound… gurgling? I try to move my ears and listen hard, but I can't wiggle them. I never could. Uncle Yany, Paul's brother, could. Maybe I am simply dead and if I am, I should be able to talk to the dead, right? Now I try to move my feet. When you're dead, you can't move or even think. Dead people can't think. I'm yelling to see if anything happens. "Yany, Yany, are you here? Paul, are you here?" No, Yany is not here, Paul is not here. Nobody's answering. I listen hard. And now I hear; ayuda, it's louder now. Sounds like ayudante. Now I can hear some more gurgling sounds in the back. I can hardly make them out. Socorro… socorrooooo. Someone's in trouble, screaming for help? Or is that an animal, maybe a wolf?

So, I'm not alone.

I'm looking down now as far as I can, towards my belly. I try to put air in my lungs and stick out my stomach… tilt my head forward … I can only tilt my head one degree, maybe two, because my head is in a rack or a metal ring? My chin can't reach my chest. I can't lean forward. Am I shackled to this stone chair?

It sure as hell feels like my hands are in cuffs and chained to the stone. I can't lean back either. Perhaps I can strain my eyes a little lower so I can see into my lap. Is there a sack on my head and I am looking through ragged holes? I can't strain my neck too much because it hurts. I can see my knees though. I have black pants on. Have I got any black pants? I must have. Do I have a broken neck? I don't think so. If my neck were broken, I wouldn't be able to move my head at all. I have to think…

I was all dressed up to meet Olly, but now I'm wearing black pants and from what I can see I have an eight wheeled personnel carrier silkscreened in color on the front of my T-shirt. I can't see any company name, just a picture of a green personnel carrier. I suck my teeth. I don't wear T-shirts with armored vehicles on them! But at least I can turn my head sideways and up a little and I can focus my eyes. I'm in pain when I move my head forward even if just a little, but my head's definitely in a metal rack. I can move it a few degrees in either direction. Have I got a spinal injury? Would I feel that? Would it hurt like arthritis? I know arthritis can be terribly painful. So, my wrists and my legs are restrained with a little movement and I can still wiggle a little. Why can't I move my arms? Are they broken? They are not strapped by my side but to a chain to the back of this rock and I can only lift them about six inches. My arms aren't paralyzed they are just restricted. That's what it is, restricted. I can move my fingers and I can close my hands into a fist. I am trying to touch the side of my pants with my fingers and feel the material. These could be jeans, because there is a seam on both sides.

That fire must be past the body, and it is burning along happily… a happy little fire we're having here, a Japanese person would say. This is not a joke! I am thinking of Hiroshima, Nagasaki, and Chernobyl… my nephew Saba… radiation from Chernobyl killed him. Why am I thinking of my nephew? I have my own problem right now. Maybe I'm thinking of him out of compassion.

Let's find out what else hurts. My elbows hurt when I want to bend them more or straighten them. I can bend both. I can move them close to my body, move them up a little and down a bit. I have metal cuffs on and the same goes for my legs. If I could straighten my legs, I could get up. So, actually I don't really know if I could bend my knees more than 5 to 10 degrees. I don't know if they would hurt if I wanted to straighten them. My legs too are manacled to this rock. Throat is okay but I have this sour taste in my mouth and my stomach feels like I ate aluminum or something with too much Monosodium Glutamate. I usually get that metallic feeling in my stomach when I eat out in a restaurant. I hear Ayuda, ayuda…

Did I eat out? I had ham and eggs this morning. This morning? What morning? Did I have an appointment in the morning with this man, Olly? Or have I been working for him already? I don't think I had lunch; I'd remember that. My last meal I remember having was in the morning, some morning.

Now I feel a whiff of air, but it isn't coming from the burning corpse, or I'd recognize the smell of burning human flesh. Could it have been an aerial robot flying by? A quadcopter? This is a bummer. I can only remember having breakfast downstairs at my apartment at Jo-Jo's and leaving the restaurant. I don't have to pee, thank God. Luckily, I don't have to defecate either.

There is fog in my head and my memory is blurred. My headache is easing and now I remember segments from my past. The fire is hissing and burning like dynamite or gunpowder. After the war, when I was just a kid, I used to play with ammunition, and it burned the same way. The eerie sound forces me to look towards the dead body. Along with the fire behind the guy's gut, nothing has changed. The shoe bothers me, though. It appears to be a black shoe. Maybe it is dark brown. I can't make out the heel on it. Shoe heels can tell a lot about a person. They could be flat footed, handicapped, a military man, a young man or an old man. He wasn't a dry-waller for sure, or the shoe would be covered in plaster. Was he a truck driver? No, but maybe a security guard. Yes, of course. He could have been that, but they don't have people watching properties anymore. What properties am I thinking about? Was I at this man's factory when this explosion or something happened? Surveillance is all done by GPS now. Then who the heck was he, or was he? I am trying to force myself to think about the job I got or not got. I think I got it, though.

So, if I got the job, was I a programmer? Was I working in sales? Was I selling ammunition, or weapons in Africa, the Middle East, Mexico, or Venezuela? Perhaps in the USA or Canada? Ordinary people still use handguns. If I could reach into my pocket and look into my passport, I could at least find out what country I'm in. But I can't reach into my pocket, my elbows won't bend! Not only that, I don't even know which pocket my passport is in. Maybe it was in my jacket inside pocket, if I had a jacket on. I took my passport out and gave it to somebody… But I don't even have a jacket on. It wouldn't be in my pants pocket. Why would I have my passport with me, anyway? And it's not likely since I am wearing a T-shirt. You don't wear a jacket with a T-shirt. This is not the US or Canada for sure. I am thinking hard now. I am licking my lips. There must be an opening for my mouth in this sack, if I'm wearing one. Is this a potato sack, orange sack or a sack made for heads? My lips are dry and cracked and they taste like soot. I don't have a beard, only stubbles, moustache, I can only lick stubbles under my nose. I extend my tongue as far as I can. I draw a deep breath through my nose and let it out. I don't think I have anything on my face, or I'd feel it when I blow upwards. I am slightly dizzy from the rush of oxygen in my lungs. There's oxygen in the air and probably pollutants as well. Let me see if I can hold my breath until I count to a hundred. I have to give up at thirty-four. I've got to do something to make time pass. It's not dark, just nebulous. Is this day or night? Is there someone behind me? There must be. That's where the desperate sounds came from.

Do I glow at night? Am I radioactive? How long can a person live with radiation sickness? A week, a month? I'll starve to death in ten days if I don't die of thirst first. Is there hope that someone will come along and rescue me? Not a chance. This is not normal! No one can be that close to a fire that burns all day and not catch on fire itself.

Ayuuudaaaa… someone is screaming from afar. The sounds are coming from behind me. Someone must be hollering for help. I think I am just dreaming! I keep telling myself that. But if I'm in the abyss of hell, am I at the edge of hell or am I in it half ways? Am I sitting on a ledge of hell, like on the edge of a swimming pool paralyzed? But then, I shouldn't be hearing myself hollering yet, I do. I did hear myself hollering to Yany. I can hear my own words. I can faintly hear sounds, voices in the rear. I am pretty sure I'm awake and sure as heck I am alive. So, then what I'm seeing is real, for sure. So, how did I wind up being here on this block of stone and attached to it and paralyzed? I don't think I'm paralyzed, though. Someone has brought me here and put me in this metal rack. They will have to come back and check on me to see if I'm still alive. I can move my legs a little and feel them.

*****

Now something is harkening back… I was paid out, everybody was. The company I worked for quit the business. Do I have a government job now? Was I working for the government? I don't know. I have to think, I seem to be confused… Was I let go from my new government job? Governments don't let important programmers go. With computer-related jobs exploding I knew I would find a job pretty fast, especially since I was the company's top programmer. I must have been working for a private company. Am I dwelling on something that happened years ago, or imagining that a dozen of us were decoding rockets aimed at various armed forces all over the world? No! That was before! I am getting mixed up again.

I seem to remember a couple weeks after my company closed, I was offered a position by somebody named Olly. That's it. We had exchanged a few emails. This employer had even called me on my smartphone. See, it's coming back again! He emailed me a set of numbers to decode that no one else could do. I have memorized the numbers 2,5,7,9,12,14,15,19,23,23,25,30,30,7,9,10 ,22,25,26,8,9,18,20,27,7,28,13,16,16.

I knew there was no 11, 21, 24 and 29. Those four sets of numbers would have altered the command greatly. The numbers had nothing to do with pi – 3.14159265 I'm telling myself that my mind is working! So then let's get to it. Let's see if I can dig into my mind and start from the time, I picked up my severance cheque. I was getting ready to go to my friend's apartment to play cards. This must have happened recently. Something is coming back I can see the date on my calendar, it was August the 14^{the} a Thursday. I know it was that day because I always played cards, 'shoot' on Thursday afternoons with the boys at their apartment. I won a lot of hands on that day; the cards were running. Something more is coming back. There was four of us; Rip, Kindy, Rudy and me. But today is Friday, the day after cards…I know, I am in a bar the 'Red Onion' I'm having a bottle of beer and I'm thinking of the message in the numbers I had just decoded. I am walking home from the Brantford General Hospital. It is 11:30 pm and my face is all bandaged up with barely enough room for my eyes to open. I had been in a fight. I was standing at the bar, yeah, having a beer, a Canadian, when a stripper approached me and asked me if I wanted a table dance. I said no. Then this tough guy, who was standing beside me, probably the stripper's pimp, elbowed me in the ribs and asked me if she wasn't good enough for me. I said I had other things on my mind, which I did. It's not that I didn't want to tell him to piss off, I wanted to; but I noticed there were three or four of them in a group. But then the bugger sucker punched me. He hit me on the side of my head. With my right fist I hit him back.

He went down like a sack. I had him on the floor and just before I hammered his head once more, another guy grabbed my arm and kicked me in the ribs. He was most likely a member of the group. That kick took my breath away for a couple seconds, just long enough for me to see a third guy kicking me in the face. That hurt. I staggered back knocking my head hard against a post. I regained my footing and straightened up and hit the third guy with my right, square in the jaw which must have rattled his teeth. His teeth rattled alright, and his mouth bled and while he was spitting about a half of dozen of his teeth onto the floor, his blood sprayed out his mouth like water from a pressure washer. I didn't get any on me. I must have ruptured an artery. The second guy jabbed me again, this time in the stomach, which I defused a little with my left arm. Then I caught him with a right hook, not too strong though because the first guy got hold of a chair and hit me in the head with it. That concussed me. As I was falling, someone grabbed me and that's when the cops arrived. The police put some guys in cuffs, but they took me to the Brantford General Hospital. The paramedics carried the guy without his front teeth outside and sent him some place else. I told the cops I didn't start the fight, and they said they knew that. They had written down my MO and a doctor in the emergency department stitched me up and asked me if I needed a ride home. I told him I lived near by in the Terrace Hill Street tower and I could walk home.

My smartphone broke in the fight. I took a Tylenol with a beer and sat down in front of my computer. There was an email from Olly he wanted to meet with me. Ah ha, this is the person with the numbers. I must have given him the right answer. He wanted to meet me in person on Wednesday which was okay with me because I knew I'd be healed up by then. He said his factory was in Brantford, along Highway 403 just east of Rest Acres Road. I remember that place being built, and I always wondered what it was going to be. He didn't want to see me at his plant, but in a park by an old pedestrian bridge over the Grand River behind the Brantford casino.

This was the time I met Olly, my new employer. That was at the beginning. Things are coming together now. The suit, the tie. He had cautioned me not to come with a wire or any other device. I wonder why he was telling me that. I wasn't about to record anything. Of course, he wouldn't have known that. I wasn't a spy working for another company, and I wasn't going to steal any information. I was looking for employment. Plain and simple. I know I was a pretty good programmer.

Did I tell him I spoke four languages and have been all over the world, including the Middle East? Did he find me on the net? I don't think I'm on the net. Maybe I am now. My old company might have put him on to me by trying to help me find a job. Did he check out my past? He must have!

Did he know I used to belong to the OPS Group (Optimal Precaution System Group) which is an international operation that reports daily on important happenings in the air, land and seas? Not likely, but if he did, he should have also known I was a top programmer who had been in Bosnia and Benghazi and had seen bombings all around the world. He should have known I had witnessed death and destruction; people being blown up and he should have known I saw individuals die with their family around them. He should have been aware of my knowledge of how to defeat rogue computer hacks, programs that guide drones, aerial robots like batbuts and roachbuts and he must have known that I was well versed in the five D's; 'destroy, deny, degrade, disrupt and deceive'. And that's what I used exclusively against terrorist groups. Did some terrorists put me here? Did they want to kill me, burn me alive in a fire? That's possible. My own three D-s, desire, determination, and drive, must have really meant something to him. But now I'm sitting on this stone and how did I get here, how? Who did this to me? Was I on fire?

I dressed up in my Sunday best when I went to see him. I drove to the Brantford casino, and I found an empty spot and parked the car.

Then I walked to the end of the building. There was a rusty old pedestrian bridge, and a decommissioned railroad station when I saw him.

He was smirking... I am losing it again, hang on relax! I'm telling myself. Where was I operating from? Where did he send me? Where did I go? I think I was going after a person who was silent jamming somebody from somewhere in a remote place. I should have lots of money on me... Dollars, Euros... I seem to remember the distant past but my short-term memory is in and out. Is my brain messing with me again? Okay... let's go back to jamming. It is flashing back now, I was in a cyber war, developing a counterattack on a spurious loud source. First, I had to search for the adversary. I might have been in the US, Russia or China? I don't think I would have wasted time on creating anti-jamming programs for passenger planes. Good practice though. Passenger planes are sitting ducks. They can be brought down with hand-held rockets. Who was I concentrating on? The source I was looking for had to be a 'wannabe', a guy, a gal... What the heck, I could be classified as a wannabe, or I could have been if Olly hadn't found me. Maybe I still am, if I can't figure out how to get myself out of this situation. So, the attack was loud... just to throw programmers off, making them think their system was compromised... like the old days of spies and counter spies, double agents, white spies, and black spies. Today we are vying for the same results but with different means. I don't know if I was doing this on my own or was, I already working for him?

Did Olly give me this job? It must have been Olly! I must have been working on a case for Olly. He had given me the job! But why am I thinking about the old days' white spies versus black spies? Perhaps because I was one of them for such a long time?

17

Here I go with the old stuff again… when I bought my girls a packman; I recall losing every game I played against them. Why, because they were quicker, and their thoughts were ahead of mine. I could see that and when I began using my own method, I started winning. But I didn't win all the time. When I started second guessing the machine's next move, I won every time. I used Gretzky's system 'think about where the puck is going to be not where it has been'. This is the way I operate now and whatever I do, I win! And that is what Olly liked about me, I always win! I always guess the computer's next move. I never accept losing. So, what in heck am I doing sitting, or being glued to this stone? I don't think I'm glued to it though. And now I can't think any more… I am putting my brain in a vice and cranking the screw. My brain is hurting. I must get into survival mode! Breathe deep, inhale, exhale… inhale, hold it for a ten count, exhale repeat. Was I tortured? I think I could have been because I ache all over. It's a steady ache in my arms and legs, like I'm hooked to low voltage electricity. The burning dude must have been tortured, but he's dead. I see no blood stains on my T-shirt or on my knees, at least in the front. The vice is squeezing the heck out of my brains… was I in Ukraine and working for the Russians? Was I in North Korea? I am thinking.

Anyway, it makes no difference who gave me the job, unless… I was working for Olly already, he'll come and free me! I am here now! My grandfather used to tighten the screw on his grape press and the juice would be squeezed out between the slats. Paul used to help him. I can see… no, I can feel a whole bunch of zeros and one's flowing out in between the slats. All I have to do is arrange them properly. I could use some of grandfather's wine right now. The tub is filling up with zeroes and ones. Somebody is dumping the grape juice into a vat. Is it Paul? The zeroes and ones are fermenting… There are men with wooden ten-gallon containers strapped to their backs, dumping the grapes into grandpa's press. Other than the irritating whooshing sound

18

coming from the body, now I can hear the broken cries from the rear, ayudaaaa… I think this means help – in Spanish? From here it looks like the burning body is smack in the middle of a gas pipe or oil pipe and his body is the wick. The fire is in his gut. That's what it is. I still have to get out from this metal band around my waist.

Here come the zeroes and the ones again… My short-term memory is returning. But what's happening? Is this Olly? I am calling out his name. Is Olly coming to help me? I don't hear anything from the rear now.

CHAPTER THREE

We are behind the Elements casino in Brantford, so I greet him and he says "hi" and we shake hands. Now I hear a buzz, am I imagining things? My mind is playing tricks on me. As I sit here on this stone, I am happy that I still have my hearing. It is not a buzz it is a low hissing sound, like air or gas escaping from a pipe. The sound is coming from the burning corps' direction. It could be gas. Olly's hand is warm, as if he had it in his pocket. Gosh, I'm thinking not another one! I used to work for a man who played pocket hockey every time he walked down the office aisle and with his 'zu' glasses he could see what was happening behind him. There were ten, fifteen open cubicles on one side of the aisle and most of them were occupied by young women. Sometimes when they changed position, they'd spread their legs revealing their panties. He'd get a charge out of that. He was hoping to see a young woman without panties. He was a pompous dude pining to be admired by all the female employees.

Now Olly jerks me back to reality.

I am confused… where the heck am I now? The guy with the zu glasses is in my *long-term* memory!

This is real, he greets me; "Good to see you Charles, I want us to be on a first name basis, so you just call me Olly. Never call me boss, mister so and so, just call me Olly. And I'll call you Charles, is that okay with you?"

"Sure Olly."

"Now listen to me Charles, you like to be called Charles, right? Not Chuck, Chas, or Chucky?"

"Right Olly."

"Nothing on you Charles?"

"Nothing Olly."

"Mind if I check?"

"Not at all Olly, go ahead." I am reaching air with both of my hands.

"You don't have to do anything Charles, I'll just push this button in my pocket. You have to keep your hand in your pocket when you scan somebody. I'll get you one of these too. I could have winked at you. That would also have activated my scanner, but it would have given you the wrong impression of me. You're not my type of Charles."

I was okay with that.

But if I'm going to work for him, I should be up to date with all the gadgets, I thought. I could see why he had his hand in his pocket. If he had winked, I could have thought he was blinking, or worse… was hitting on me.

"So, Charles, have you ever been tortured?" This question shocked me. Starting a conversation this way is weird. To me torturing began with pulling out fingernails and other physical kinds of tortures. Some special techniques, perfected in the twenty-first century.

He was asking this while facing me and putting his right hand on my shoulder. When he touched me a minute electric shock raced through my body down to my feet, but I didn't let on. I didn't want him to know I felt anything. I almost shivered though, because I imagined myself sitting in a sauna and someone coming in with cold slimy hands and touching my naked body. But I shivered in my mind only because I wasn't going to show him, I resented his touch.

Unblinking, I looked him in the eyes. He had grey eyes, a light grey which almost blended with his orbs. My eyes could have still been bloodshot from the fight, I don't know.

His eyes glanced down on the front of my pants thinking his touch made me pee myself. Actually, when he touched my shoulder, I did have a reaction in my sphincter, (women have kegels) people pee or even crap themselves under extreme interrogation.

Sadists know that torture hurts only the living. Once you're dead, you don't feel anything. How do I know that?

I have died several times and I've never felt any pain, or even a sensation. Three times I was hit by lightning, and I drowned three times. And once I was electrocuted. In the moment I died, I never saw any virgins or God or anything.

I would suggest to you to die when you are tortured. Then you don't feel a thing. But to Olly my reply was; "no Olly, I have never been tortured." I thought about Walter Gretzky's cousin in Poland during the war. He was a partisan; he was caught tortured and killed.

I said to Olly I was aware of the fact that most tormentors knew if you died you didn't feel anything anymore. They don't expect you to know what it feels like to be tortured. When they are cutting your fingers off one by one the best thing to do is black out instantly.

Even the thought of being tortured gave me the creepers.

Some inhuman barbarians take you to the threshold of your life by pulling your fingernails out until you faint. Then they wait until you come around and continue cutting your fingers off, one by one. It is best if you die, not just faint, but die. Then it's over. There is no more pain, and you don't feel a thing. What you have to know though is how to come back from the dead.

My history teacher used to tell us his version of medieval tortures.

After each episode he enjoyed the expression on our faces. For months I couldn't fall asleep. I thought about the people who had died on the cross or on the rack or in the 'chair'. Then there was the dunking, pre curser of water boarding. Then there was the boiling, the freezing, and the live burial. The teacher must have invented his own stories about people being thrown to hungry rats, tigers, or hyenas.

I of course, was never tortured because I was never captured. I think I'm being tortured now. While I waited for Olly's next question, the 'dungeons of Iran' flashed through my mind. That was a very depressing thought. Surely, he wasn't taking me for a pussy cat, and surely, he wasn't going to hire me to torture people. Actually, I didn't know what he wanted me for. I was hoping for employment in cybernetics. He must have had a definite reason to say the things he said. He must have been leading me in a certain direction and getting at something... Every word he used sounded deliberate. In any case, I reassured him I hadn't been tortured.

"When I put my hand on your shoulder, did you feel anything Charles?"

Now I had to answer him honestly. Should I lie? No, I had better tell the truth. If I lied, he'd know, and I'd be screwed, this job would be over. I had no reason to lie anyway!

"I did Olly, I felt a very low voltage on my shoulder, far less than static electricity." And that was the truth, because I had been shocked by living room carpets before. They make you jump.

"We've got to fix that. You shouldn't have been feeling anything on your shoulder. Did you feel a slight pressure on your prostate gland like you had to pee?" he asked in a deliberate way. Actually, I did feel something like that... but now... how in heck... I'm losing it again. I am losing it! Inside my head now I have a screen just like a broken TV. I see wiggly black lines running horizontally, vertically, diagonally. I feel nauseated and the metallic taste in my mouth is back. I don't know what is real, being strapped onto this blackened cinderblock or meeting with Olly. Am I being tortured now?

Suddenly Olly seems to materialize. He is about my height, 5 foot ten, about the same weight, but I am in better shape. I know that. I am tough. He doesn't look tough to me. Age wise, he might be 50 or 60 years old, or perhaps 150 or 160, I can't tell. We are all up there in age, I am thinking. Age doesn't matter anymore. If your brain is capable to carry you on, that's the most important thing.

If you can create and figure things out, you are relevant at any age. That's what's important, you must stay relevant. You're either capable to do the task you are given or not. Your ability, your style is the thing that qualifies you for the job.

Now-a-days we can live as long as we want to, as long as we stay healthy. Health is important. We must eat the right kind of food and exercise, even the brain. Especially the brain, you've got to keep your brain happy. Think about neuroplasticity – gray matter. That is your brain. If you're a politician, a teacher, or a scientist, the harder the job for your brain the better.

Olly's face has a shade of grey to it, certainly not tanned. His voice is sharp, military style, and slightly British accented, but I don't think he is British. He is in a grey tweed jacket, with a grey shirt and grey pants with no tie. His shoes are grey too and look comfortable – Italian, perhaps. Grey eyes grey shirt, grey everything, very impressive. His handshake is firm, he has longer than normal fingers. He might be a piano player. His hands are not tanned. He is not a golfer.

"Do you have any preference as to where you want to work? I mean in what country would you prefer to work from?"

Now, why is he questioning me like this? We are in Canada, what's wrong with working in Canada or working from right here? My previous job was in the Iroquois Complex in Brantford on Wayne Gretzky Boulevard. Gretzky is more famous than Graham Bell was, and he invented the telephone. It didn't matter to me where I worked, my kids were all grown up and they were living in different cities. None of them lived here and as far as I know none of my grandkids lived here either. Most of them I wouldn't recognize, anyway. I don't even remember some of my own kids. I'm not married, and I'm not tied to anyone now. Brantford is fine with me.

I have worked in New York, Boston, and Mobile Alabama, maybe that's why he was asking. Actually, I could work from anywhere. He might have thought I wanted to be close to my family. Or maybe he thought I had young grandkids I could train for programmers. They would have expertise from the games they played on their pads. Should I lie… tell him I have young children. I am up there in age too, but I look like I am fifty – 46? He probably knows how old I really am and maybe I could ask him how old he was, if I was that interested, but I wasn't.

"It all depends on the job, Olly, no?" I said, acting somewhat surprised.

"You are one hundred percent right Charles, although as you know an adversary's location is seldom known for sure. You could be working in a large city, a capital or in a jungle," he said as he was looking at me and squinting.

"As long as you have internet and a super laptop with near unlimited power you can work from anywhere."

I had some acquaintances in other countries, maybe relatives too or perhaps even children, or ex-wives but this position does not look like I'd want to bother any of my relations with it. I could have people working for me, although I have never supervised more than forty people at a time and that was in my younger days.

He must have been waiting for something from me. Maybe he wanted to know if I had any problem with my location or our government. I didn't know what he had in mind. I was determined to work for him and help him out. That was all.

"Look Olly, I really enjoy cybernetics and the sort, wherever I'm located. I do what needs to be done. I don't concern myself too much with politics, although I usually wind up working for politicians. May I ask you a question, are you red or blue?"

"Blue, but sometimes red, it all depends. Sometimes we have to make borderline decisions, positive or negative. We have to be the 'good' guys, or the 'bad' guys. Most of the time I decide which side we are going to support." We usually go as the politicians want us to go, or sometimes the other way. He faked a grimace, or maybe it was a smile. I don't know if he smiled.

"Got you." I said.

I was meaning blue for the West, red for the East. Now that I had that out of the way, we could parley easier and from the same point of view. Red would have been a little tougher.

"In your mind Charles, how good are you?"

"Goes without saying Olly, did I figure out the numbers?"

Olly smirked with that familiar grimace like uncle Yany used to, spreading his cheeks, crunching his teeth. It almost looked like a smile... I liked that grimace. Maybe that's why I liked Olly. He was almost a dead ringer for my uncle Yany or Lindsay

Graham on Fox News who looked exactly like Yany. Within the next hour he had asked about a thousand questions that I answered, rapid-fire, without hesitation. He wasn't interested in my personal affairs, only my expectations in the future. I assured him I had planned nothing out of ordinary, I simply enjoyed and loved cybernetics. He told me about some of the projects he was working on, that were coming up or planned in the near future. I would be working with him to start.

Everything that came up from time to time, concerning computers, would be my department.

Is he going to hire me? He hasn't said anything yet.

"So, Olly what do you think? Am I your man?" I asked him and he replied, "you are going to be perfect for the job. You are tough, intrepid, experienced, and loyal. You're going to be my best friend, Charles. You're going to be not only an employee, but my best friend. How's about that Charles?"

I was blushing, in my mind. How can he call me his best friend when he doesn't even know me, or does he? How does he want me to react to that? I had to stop imagining some people I was intimate with, but that was always the opposite sex. As far as guys were concerned – I had a few close friends, like Kindy, Rudy, Rip – the guys I used to play cards with. Some guys I golfed with or went to strip clubs with. That brought up the Red Onion in my mind. I shouldn't have gone there alone.

"Charles, I checked you out and I probably know you better than your mother did. We are cyber twins Charles."

Good grief, I didn't know I had a twin but let's see what happens.

"Charles, I'll pay you three hundred thousand dollars a year on paper. That is for tax purposes. Other than that, you'll have an unlimited expense account, and ten thousand company shares which is worth at least ten million dollars and this is just between you and me only, and is in an offshore account. I'll also make a deposit for you in my bank, and I mean in *my* bank, because I own it – for one million dollars. Charles from this moment on you're a millionaire, just like me, except I am a billionaire."

I staggered.

I thought I had lost my mind. I felt like fainting, couldn't believe what he just said. I kept pinching myself, wake up Charles, wake up... He went on telling me about his parents – how they were killed in an accident when he was... and he almost said it, how old he was. They had had residences in various cities in the world, but they were German nationals, related to the Dunlops and the Kaisers, who were in the armament industry. He told me his parents were on the Concord when it went down and he paused briefly, a slight tremor swept across his face. He had no brothers or sisters, only distant useless cousins.

This was very good news for me. Generally there are family members who can create problems in a company. Often there's rivalry, jealousy, or competition for power. He told me the company's name but asked me not to talk about it too much.

In Canada, he was registered under the name of Multi Trade Resources, MTR and I would be working for that company. In the world – meaning the higher circles that he'd belonged to; he was referred to as R.Inc. (Resources Incorporated). He also spoke four languages, fluently.

"You have a car, Charles?" he asked. That threw me. I had to have come here by some vehicle, and I didn't mean sag way, but I could have come by taxi. Could have come by Uber, even though they are private drivers that could be criminals or even killers sometimes.

"I have a rental Tesla parked in the casino lot. A guard noticed me walking out of the rear parking lot and asked me if I was coming back to the casino because parking was provided for customers only. All other vehicles would be towed. I lied. I told her I would be coming back."

This bothered me because if I hadn't come back into the casino, there would be a permanent black spot on my image forever. I'm not a gambler. That's a job all to itself.

I said this to Olly while my head became a beehive again and the bees started flying everywhere. This can't be true I must be dreaming all of this. I can't be sitting here on a cinder block watching this guy burning and having a conversation with Olly. It's impossible.

Yet I seem to be able to stay on the subject while coping with my present situation. But sometimes I get ahead of myself and other times I get behind. Sometimes I get all mixed up.

Through a hazed mind I hear Olly calling me, "Charles…"

I answer, "I don't like to leave a besmirched profile of myself Olly. At least I should go inside the casino to erase my image from the parking violator's list." This was a logical decision.

"Got you Charles, let's go in and have a sandwich. I don't do any gambling, with my money that is," he said, and gave me a Yany.

I had this unbelievable offer from Olly that blew my mind. A million bucks… the thought by itself made me dizzy, let alone the ten thousand shares in his company.

We went through the front door where a uniformed guard took a passing look at us and turned to assist an elderly woman who couldn't find the 'up' button for the elevator. He must have noticed me because he did something to his smartphone.

We are walking up the steps to the cafeteria where I'm ordering a beer and a BLT. Olly orders a BLT only. I am looking around, but I don't see anyone I know, and I am certain no one would have known Olly or me either. Our image would be erased in a week but not from the encrypted bank. There now I do exist, and so does Olly, and we both live there forever. Now he is talking about his plant and the products he makes.

Was this the time I dressed up to meet him? Yes.

We are sitting at a table at the Elements Casino in Brantford and Olly starts up with a Yany on his face, "Charles, among many other things, I am in the *designer* war business. We make armaments and ammunitions, and we have testing facilities for small arms underground, and for new weapons in different countries. We are working with labs all over the world to come up with antidotes, medicines, and vaccines against viruses or possible pandemics. We get involved with skirmishes between countries pretty much all around the world. Often, we *influence* the outcome of conflicts between regions, nations and people. We'll take orders from everywhere; Africa, Central Europe, Bosnia, Kosovo, you know what I mean Charles." He pauses as he looks at me and my necktie. He nods pleasingly.

I guess he likes my necktie. I like it too. I was thinking about his statement 'designer' war. I wasn't quite sure I understood him correctly. I thought maybe he meant arming the participants of a pre-designed war, meaning arming both sides of a conflict.

"We initiate trends in fashions too," Olly said.

I liked this part better, but made no comments about anything, just nodded. I wanted to leave the talking to him.

"We advocate leaders in countries like Mexico, Venezuela, and countries in Africa. In the US, we support the popular political parties, the Democrats and the Republicans and assist party leaders. We have backed Gaddafi and many others and voided them when the trend required change. Drug trafficking is popular now and so is people trafficking. To keep everyone busy diaspora of third world inhabitants to rich countries is important. We can't have peace for too long though because everything goes stale. Ordinary people need to work hard to achieve their goals. Ordinary people shouldn't get too wealthy because they get lazy. Ordinary people don't know how to handle money. We won't have socialism either because the wealth gets in the wrong hands – into the hands of politicians, who will squander it then when it is gone there goes socialism and the next step is communism. Get it Charles? We'll definitely not have communism. We make sure of that."

I was very, very happy about hearing that.

Holy mackerel! I couldn't swallow fast enough. Now I could see why he was making ammunition for small arms or for that matter any type of armaments, for whatever it takes to fight a conflict.

"The vehicles, planes, rockets, are made elsewhere." He said.

"We have to keep communism in check, can't allow Russia, China, Cuba and North Korea get too strong. We have to keep an eye on socialist countries too. Small armaments are needed for uprisings, skirmishes, insurgencies, revolutions and of course for local police forces. They have to be readied and distributed," he concluded.

I was astonished, but I didn't let on. He kept looking at me as if he was expected to see some physical reaction. What the hell was a big shot like Olly doing in Brantford and designing wars here none-the-less. Who are his associates, his backers, his supporters, I'm thinking to myself?

Where does he live anyway? Maybe in one of those high-rise penthouses in downtown Brantford, or maybe he's an alien. I wanted to hide my bedazzlement, but I didn't know if I succeeded. I wanted to look as cool as a cucumber. I was wondering if I should even work for him. He had to have a good reason for telling me what all his business was about. I thought he was God.

At one point when he said he was my cyber twin, I thought he was God for sure. I think I had that thought right after we went out to my car in the parking lot, and he asked me to drive him to his plant off Rest Acres Road.

*****

Rest Acres Road was under construction, and I think I was stopped by a flag man. I remember getting out of the car and thinking whoa, I smell something… it is phosphorus explosives maybe matches? Or is this coming from the burning body? Or someone is lighting a cigarette or pipe with a match? If that was it, I'd smell the tobacco too, on grandfather's breath, phosphorus…? I must have been jerked back for an instance to the body that *is* burning with an eerie whoosh. Why am I back here now? Because I'm trying to get out of these pants. See, if I could only stand up… little by little I could try to put weight on my right foot but had no result. I don't feel my feet or the ground; my feet are numb. I try my left foot. Nothing. There is a steady 'cramping' sort of pain though and body pain all over. This is not possible. I can't be sitting upright and be paralyzed.

I must be fastened to my seat by some means. But my seat is a rectangular rock. How do I know that when I can't see myself sitting? Oh, but I did when I had that 'out of body' vision. The pressure on my temples is unbearable, I am nauseated and feel like fainting. Had I passed out and imagined seeing myself? I'm able to think! So, I haven't fainted! Now that smell is gone. Had I passed wind? Fart smells like phosphorus. God, am I getting incontinent? Is this the Third World War? If that's the case, I am in deep trouble. No one can survive this one, not even Olly. I must keep moving even if only a little at a time. Very slowly I am trying to move my toes… right foot, big toe – big toe, move you bugger! I can't feel any movement, I must try harder. Left toes aren't moving either. Holy Moly, here comes the phosphorous smell again. Very light, it's got to be a match. The smell has got to be coming from the side or the rear because I still can't smell the burning body which is in front of me.

Who's behind me? I hear fading strangling words again like 'socorro, scocorrroooo, ayuda, ayuda. Someone's got to be calling for help.

Am I back with Olly? I holler his name in fear again and again, wait. I don't hear an answer. I ask, 'who's there'? I ask again, but still no answer I just hear a faint word that sounds like ayuda.

I'm getting annoyed now. I try to move my shoulders and realize I can move them upwards and down a little, but very slowly! Boy oh boy, has anybody ever been in this situation, I'm guessing not. I am going to die here, frozen to this black stone. Now I am confusing reality with the past again. But what is reality? I am sitting down and can't move, that is reality.

Olly's calling me now, "Charles, Charles…"

I get it. When I got out of the car, I smelled some construction worker lighting up a cigarette. That's where the phosphorous smell came from.

"I was just looking," I said to Olly. "They're making an elaborate intersection to your plant," I remarked.

"It's about time," Olly said as he too stepped from the car. "I made an agreement with Brantford four years ago. I got three hundred acres of land for free, I don't know if you're interested in this…"

Of course, I wasn't, but I didn't interrupt him because he was talking about employees and having only engineers on contract and no workers in the shop was odd as hell. What good does he do for Brantford? I pondered.

But that was just my opinion. Maybe he pays high taxes, I don't know. He must have guessed my thoughts because he said he paid taxes like everyone else. But the bulk of the money is paid though the business.

"There are other benefits for the city," Olly went on.

"We contract technicians to maintain our automated machines.

We finance research and development in the city. We use local machine shops; high-tech industries and we sponsor new learning additions to the Wilfred Laurier College and the new building of the Long Boat College in Ohsweken. In the past years the population in Ohsweken had increased greatly because a lot of indigenous people with young families had moved here from various remote parts of Canada. Some had even come from the states, from Dakota. Higher education was offered free for indigenous students who were ambitious and qualified for universities. Those who chose 'higher' learning were given zero interest loans and were encouraged to settle in Brantford. We've added another landing strip to the Brantford airport.

We are building a brand-new spaceport just north of Brantford. The government is expanding Metro from Toronto, all the way to London Ontario right under our feet.

We are a magnet for high-tech people in this Silicone Valley north, or as it is often called in the native language, Tunngasugit (means welcome in Inuktitut). A win-win situation," he said.

I agreed with all of that and nodded.

"Charles, ah… if I asked you to hire fifteen school children, mainly boys, 2-3 hours a week between twelve to fourteen years old, where would you find them? You'd give the kids projects, competitive games for instance; the easiest way to catch a rabbit or how to create a new game with a football. They would have to develop the activities themselves. They must use their own ideas, nothing that's already available on their I-pods. Have them build simple structures towers and bridges.

If they want to, they can use animals, birds or devices whatever. Do you think you could get them to do something like that?

Do you understand what I mean Charles? What we want to see is how they approach simple *tasks, subjects* and how they apply their little minds to solve problems. Where would you find these youngsters, Charles?"

What is this? Now we're talking about children, kids in school. This must be happening in another time, I tell myself. I'm trying to connect my thinking. Am I already working for Olly?

As I stand here and process my thoughts, I think I have the job already, for sure. But that question stunned me.

He must be testing me.

I had no idea he wanted me to work with children. I had to think really fast. Is he going to pay these kids? And if so, how much?

I asked him this, and he replied, "Whatever you think is fair, money is a non-issue for us Charles. The jobs we do are worth hundreds of millions, and we can spend as much as we want. You find the kids and decide how much we should pay them. And I'm not talking about child labor either, it's child's play. While they play, they can give us great ideas.

Since you are going to look after the 'operations' you can hire instructors. You can hire professors, teachers or entertainers and pay them good wages. A thousand a day is fair. If they can help the kids think, innovate or invent, then they are priceless.

Don't you think, Charles?"

Ah ha, here comes the bulk of my job – *operations*. I was going to look after the operations. The things that I don't yet know can be the kicker. I can handle kids, adults, anyone. I'm thinking how much the government pays per day for technical help. He said a thousand, two? I didn't know. I just had to find out.

Olly continued, "You can pay the professionals twenty-five hundred if you feel it's necessary. Klutch had always paid them well."

Who is this Klutch, I thought. "Good help is hard to find, and I don't care what country you find the kids. We can take our time, three weeks, six weeks, or two months. Some jobs are timeless Charles," he said. I must ask him who this Klutch guy is.

A road grader is backing up making beeping noises I can hardly hear Olly. There was a water truck in the ditch that had gone too close to the edge of the road. This happens all the time. It takes a pretty good driver to keep a spray in line, the right distance from the ditch is critical, especially when he's driving in reverse, which is about half the time. The fresh gravel has to be soaked before the roller comes to pack it down.

"We need smart kids, Charles. Young minds can comprehend many things we adults don't even think of. We need kids that can learn fast, figure things out and chose ways, innovate, invent, and actually *make* decision under pressure. I know what you're thinking. Why didn't I get Klutch to find the kids? Because I think you'll have better ideas. Klutch is not an idea man. He's a hard worker though, and he likes to get into the thick of things.

He likes to get his hands dirty. Klutch couldn't figure out the numbers. Don't misunderstand me, Klutch is a gem! He knows everything else. You are an engineer, a problem solver. You can come up with hypothetical situations. Think up a *problem* with a situation and present it to the kids. See what they can do with it. We can watch how they approach the problem. All you have to do is make it interesting for them. Make a game of it. See who can come up with a winning strategy to solve a problem. I'm sure you know how to approach problems!

But we must win, in everything we do! It's imperative, nothing else matters. We must win in everything we do!"

I understood the meaning in 'we must win in everything we do'. But I told him in this country all kids go to school, and they all have parents.

"There are laws against child labor."

"Oh, I know that, Charles. But as I said before, you hire kids to play. You're a smart guy, all you've got to do is find a country where you can work with the kids and give them some ideas that they are going to use in their play. A foreign country is fine too like Klutch did, he had Philippine children working for him one time 'designing bridges'. They made bridges from steel, stones, ropes, all kinds of materials.

However, the children should speak English. They can use their daily homework and apply it to their 'play'. You will give them the crux, the essence of the game. As we work on many different projects, you'll have to come up with a new theme for each event. Do you get my drift, Charles? As I said before, this is play, the children will get money to play. A key word in the game is what matters! From time to time I will give you a concept the children can work on. We will record and analyze the games they design and build around their play. Get it, Charles? They'll go to school to learn – to play!"

Who is this guy Klutch, Klutch, Klutch, I wondered?

Olly carried on; this one time the schoolkids made bridges of popsicle sticks and craft sticks, glued them together. Klutch arranged assembly lines where they had to finish the project in a set time and in a competitive way. The kids were divided into A and B teams. When A team made a mistake a bell rang, and when team B made a mistake jingle-bells started to play.

Klutch structured groups of ten kids working in separate rooms. They worked on projects made with computers and printed them out and assembled them by hand. He even got a caterer who made them home cooked food with potatoes, wieners, onions, paprika and macaroni. The kids loved that food and ate it like little pigs, he said. They craved the stuff and wanted to eat the same food every day. He bought them Coca Cola to drink."

Olly went on, "some kids smoked but they were in separate rooms and exhaled the smoke into 'special filters' hanging from the ceiling. Klutch said some kids had started smoking when they were eight years old."

How old was I when I started smoking? I think I was about ten. That was the time I found a heap of abandoned ammunition in the bushes behind grandpa's wheat field. My friends and I did crazy things with those explosives. When someone came up with a new idea, like feeding cordite through tunnels, we jubilated. Sometimes we laid them end to end twenty feet long then lit one end. Cordite was like spaghetti or pickup-sticks but burned like rows of sparklers on fire.

"I got your drift, Olly." I said.

I knew how to win; I just didn't know how to design new games for children. If there was nothing pressing, I could probably come up with something unique.

But, but now I'm losing it again… my head has started to ache again. Not like a headache, but like an expanding sort of pain. It's like when I eat too much and my stomach bulges. I'm getting pretty dehydrated. Am I getting delusional, confused? I feel my skull hasn't got enough room for my thoughts and my brain wants to spill out.

My mind is back on the cinder block. Do I have a bandana on my head made of steel? Or is that just a part of the ring welded to the bar behind my back? I'm rolling my eyes upwards, but I can't see past my eyebrows. I'm trying to contain my brains at will but it's not working. It feels like I'm losing zeroes and ones. They are dripping from my eyes. Am I crying and feeling zeroes trickling down my face? Am I feeling sorry for myself? I think it's raining, sprinkling… and it is rain that's rolling down my cheeks.

Slowly, as I sit here on this damn cinder block, I am communicating with my brains again. Drip, drip, drip, I'm challenging myself.

It really hurts to think. What would kids be learning in grades five, six or seven in school now-a-days? History? Ancient history? Recent history? Churchill, Stalin? How about recent heroes – have we got any national heroes today? We have billionaires like Rupert Murdoch, Soros, Bezos, Gates and Zuckerberg. They may not be heroes, but they will be part of our history. They all have visions, and they are all famous, even though they are not yet classified as heroes. Perhaps they'll be deemed heroes in time by historiographers.

We can't use existing games because they have copyrights, but I could draw from my own experiences.

When Olly talks about Klutch he speaks as if I had known Klutch all my life. Klutch in my mind has two heads, a slim yet muscular body, four arms, two of which are wings that can flutter like hummingbird wings and muscular legs that can out pace cars. I can actually picture the pair of heads that are normal in size and quite handsome.

Since we have aliens here on earth, they could be from different planets, two heads wouldn't be all that unusual.

I visualize Klutch talking to his other self. Even the name Klutch is weird because that name had to come from somewhere – automobiles or birds. Olly keeps talking about Klutch and not Klutches. So maybe he's only got one head. Now Olly tells me Klutch hired kids from abroad before. He assured me Klutch could help out with whatever I planned to do. He's very handy with tools and machinery.

I have to get to know Klutch. I wonder where he's from. He must be English, perhaps South American? But on the other hand, he could be a robot. Robots can be anything, any nationality and they can speak any language. They just use different programs, or chips depending on what planet they are visiting. On Earth they want to look like us but on other planets they may look like… whatever they look like there. Who knows? We still don't know for sure if there's another planet out there with 'humans.' Robots can last a long time, especially if they are well made. They can last indefinitely.

Robots could last forever.

"By the way, Olly, where is Klutch from? Or is he an alien?" I ask. No, Charles, he's not an alien, he is Welsh, British.

His father was Polish. His family name is Klutchowski, but he told me to just call him Klutch. Sometimes he mutters in his own language, maybe in Polish. Usually when something is above his head. That is very interesting, Charles. It has never occurred to me to ask him what he is mumbling about. I'm glad you mentioned that. But you are right, Charles, he could pass for an alien too anybody could, even you, Charles. Are you an alien?" I looked at him.

In my mind, I thought Olly was an alien.

"Some aliens are white, some are tanned, some are metallic, and it is hard to tell what part in of the universe they are from," Olly declared and went on. "If there was a direction in the universe, which of course there isn't, because certain stars have gravitation and that is a force. In space you are pulled up by gravitational force, and away from that force is the other way, down."

"Maybe if we could mingle with them, Olly… however when it comes down to interact with aliens… they don't socialize with humans. You never see them eating or drinking with anyone or for that matter I can't even tell if they are breathing. They dress up like we do, and their skin tones may be light or swart. Do they define themselves by stature, or age?" "I don't know Charles. The stature of our aliens seems to be all over the place. They can be any height and come to think of it, all shades too. So, for that matter, they can also come with any amount of knowledge."

That made me wonder. So, if that's the case, why doesn't Olly get aliens to come up with games? They should be able to think of all kinds of new games. I ruminate crazily.

"Are there any alien babies or children, Olly?"

"Are you kidding me Charles, you know there aren't any child aliens. They are all *adults*. That would be cute though, wouldn't it be Charles?"

I can already picture the headline in newspapers, *Americans adopting extraterrestrial baby aliens*. Yes, every household should have one or two alien toddlers to bring up just like regular kids. They'd go to kindergarten, elementary school, middle school and high school." I chuckled and asked Olly, "would baby aliens be using diapers."

"Probably not." Olly said, looking at me very seriously.

"Then there wouldn't be any alien school kids either right Olly?"

We both laughed.

The rain comes and goes and so do my thoughts as I sit here.

My crazy mind keeps imagining things. If there are no alien babies or toddlers, they must have been manufactured in varying sizes. They could have been made last year or a century-ago or light-years-ago.

If they were made from machine parts and chips, they wouldn't be going to grade school or middle school or any school, and alien babies certainly wouldn't be using diapers.

I'm still wondering, if there were young aliens on earth, at what age would they have been called adults? Could they have learned to drive? Would they have been allowed to have guns? Would they have been able to hunt our animals, fish our waters? I don't think so.

Could they have been educated though? If they were learned, would their knowledge be put on a chip too? That chip would be called a mega chip to fit all disciplines.

"My mind tells me Olly, that these extraterrestrial aliens would have had to be a category all by themselves. On earth they might be called *ACES, (Asynchronous Coded Electronic Skin)*. They could be very knowledgeable knowing everything, like walking encyclopedias. But what would make them tick?

A battery?"

"Of course, Charles, it would have to be a battery' or batteries. They could have long lasting batteries; made of materials that we don't yet know. Something that is good for years, decades or more. And the size of their batteries could be as small as a dime or perhaps a grain of sand. I don't think they can make decisions on their own. I believe they are what they are. If they are pre-programmed to do a *specific* job, they do it and that's it. I never had anything to do with any of them Charles. Have you?"

"No Olly. I think they are way more advanced than we are, but you wouldn't know they don't show off with it. I wonder if they could belong to any political party."

"I don't think there are politics in space Charles. Only humans are connected to political parties. And then in the USA politicians have to gain status first. Then status can only be gained through power. Then you gain power with money… and so on."

This alien situation was getting a little too wild, so I laughed out loudly and asked Olly a burning question, "if they can't proliferate when they grow up Olly, how do you think they multiply?"

"They are machines, manufactured for pre-determined purposes Charles!" Olly laughed too, only with an ambivalent laugh.

When I think about aliens, even for a little while, I can actually take my mind off the rain that's accumulating under my feet. I carry on with my crazy thoughts.

Are there different kinds of aliens on earth and different nationalities? I wonder? There probably are. There could well be different aliens on different planets. I'm curious where *our* aliens came from. Since there are 'no' politics in space it is plain to see they couldn't influence our voting system, therefore they wouldn't have anything to do with our way of life. They wouldn't have anything to do with riots, lootings gang killings and certainly wouldn't be spreading fake news, or could they?

I can visualize a planet where the climate is temperate just like on earth. Tornadoes and hurricanes are under control.

They'd have plant life, insects and animals and human-like creatures with different vocations.

There would be a Supreme Ace, like Biden or Xi Jinping, or Putin, even higher than them; King of all Kings.

There would be supervisors, *'ranking aces'*. Though I must compare them to us humans because *our* aliens look a lot like humans here on earth. In their home the robots aces would be made as *adults* and made to order and as many as required for a particular task; depending always on the amount of *'hands'* needed to complete a job.

They can't be cloned because they are not born, they are manufactured mechanical machines. Obviously, machines don't have DNA.

They have no feelings or emotions, and they don't need air to breathe but they need CO_2 generators for animal life and for vegetation.

They can last year after year, century after century maybe indefinitely. If they have a job, they'd have to do the same thing over and over just like automated machines. They should never get bored, because machines don't get bored, they wear out. They could be very large and strong and never tire or they could be tiny. They could run on batteries or chips that would be replaced periodically when required.

On the other hand if they perish (if they do) they are probably disposed of as fertilizer or junk or heat source or recycled into some unknown but useful commodity.

If they were made to travel in space, they would be structured with some kind of heads, eyes, mouths or beaks, arms and legs as required to match the inhabitants of a particular planet they are made to visit. At home they could be made with bird size or lizard like heads or no heads at all. For different applications they'd have different degrees of knowledge, appendices, and programs, as required.

If they are made for use on earth, they'd have human-like heads stuffed with cotton or some plasticized matter.

Sometimes things could go wrong, like the wrong type of ace being sent to the wrong planet!

Then we could get aces with seven arms three heads or peepholes, eight legs or who knows what. On their own planet *my* semi-human aces would have an opening for feeding and voiding because *they* would eat something. Their sustenance could be some feed or solids, like minerals or something useful that is also used to feed their animals. The opening could be on any location on their bodies.

They would be semi-mortal.

I can imagine, after a while, they would wear out or they could become obsolete. But I guess they could last a long time. Their mortality would greatly depend on the job they do and how well they have been made or how well they have been maintained or looked after. They could be very agile or gentle.

I'm arguing with myself and come to a conclusion that none of this is possible here on earth because robot aces can't have feelings, they are machines. I carry on wildly anyway.

I really get stupid and imagine there must be males and females for appeasement purposes even amongst themselves and they are affectionately called 'Beautiful Playces'. Play boys and play girls. They could be slim or chubby, strong or meek. They could be knowledgeable or dumb. Here again, as required for the appeasement of a particular segment of their society. I imagine robots in clothes…

Robot female aces in bikinis…

If they are trained, some aces could be taking care of plants, animals or for other ace species – they could be caretakers or supervisors, as required. They'd have 'remedial personnel' for all disciplines. These aces would be very highly trained mechanics, engineers or doctors but they wouldn't be anything special, just different trades. Like in communism. In a communistic society there is only one class: *working class*. The rulers would be like the bees – queen bee – ranking ace, I keep thinking. These aces could be rewarded with some extra frills like access to Playces, but maybe not. In communist societies there aren't any tangible rewards just ranks.

Robot aces would be manufactured to strict tolerances and manuals automatically. They are created with a standard chip or chips.

Playces would be produced for the high-ranking aces and groomed to be beautiful.

In my mind there are numerous leaders occupying many other planets, light years apart. These leaders would get together occasionally when there is a new planet born or one that has died. The birth of a new planet could be as frequent as one per earth year, and that occasion could be celebrated with the creation of a new ranking ace. That date would be recorded and re-visited year after year (earth years).

These special events would use up a lot of resources.

For celebrations and the appeasement of ranking aces only, they'd have spectacular luminescent 'Fireworks Olympics' where common aces are not admitted. The production date of common aces is not celebrated in time-consuming events like birthdates, because that would cost too much energy. The special natural material they use for energy on their planet is finite but may be omnipresent on some other planets, like on earth? We don't yet know what that 'magic' material is. Maybe it is our oceans or our seas or our dirt, soil.

If we could find that out, that knowledge would help to bring us another step closer to the unknown.

As their science is vastly superior to ours, we could learn a lot from them. Maybe we should go to school on their planet? Impossible, maybe not! But it is yet not very likely. Today they can come here but we can't go there.

This rain is a soaker. The water is collecting at my feet pretty good.

So then if they are coming here, they must have a reason I'm thinking. They must have a reason to come here... I have to take my mind off of the rain, it is too depressing... I must go back to my reasoning. Now I'm thinking that there had to be a time, perhaps billions of years ago, after the universe was formed, that life evolved on this *other* earth-like planet. After a long time, there, and just like on earth, some kind of humans evolved. Their technical knowledge grew and through their scientific advances they invented robot aces to help them with their 'heavy lifting' and such. As they evolved even more greatly, to the pinnacle of their life, their technology became so good and perfect that it would last and last for a long time.

Then they started to run out of their energy.

The energy they had, worked well, and they thought ahead and invented scouting robots who were sent out to other planets in search of readily available energy fuel. These scouting robots used up a lot of fuel too, like we do when we go on vacation.

To travel from planet to planet in the universe the scouting robots needed massive amounts of fuel.

Eventually the robot scouts found our ancient earth that was populated with ancient humans and lots of the 'magic' material they needed for their energy. When these robots *mined* that 'magic' material and returned home, they unknowingly took with them a human disease.

Then in just a few centuries all the human-like on that *other* planet died out, only the robots remained.

These robots could not advance any further on their own. Even the smartest robot couldn't make any difference.

So, at this time the scouting robots came to see us on earth again. They couldn't find any more of the magic material and they couldn't take us back to their planet either, so they had to study us here on earth. They studied us throughout the 'ages' and waited until we've arrived at the right age – the computer age. We humans today are just right. Does this mean the *end of the human scenario? End of the world as we know it scenario?* I wonder what Olly would say, could he come up with a good answer. Again, I started to worry about the rain and the burning body in front of me.

Charles, Charles…I hear Olly calling, I answer; "let's just talk about this a little bit Olly. Let's go back to the beginning, to the period when humankind had all died out on this earth-like planet due to some of our contagious diseases, and the extraterrestrial robots, the *aces,* realized they were in big trouble – they started visiting us more often right Olly? They tried to take us 'home' right?"

"Yes, I think that's what happened Charles."

"The robots 'the machines' were not prone to diseases themselves, but they unknowingly took the molecular virus home and infected their human-like makers with something like COVID-19. The alien robots were impervious to the disease, but

48

they could have been 'carriers'. Now that they are here, Olly, what do you think they want from us? Do they want our vaccine, or they want to relearn our human ingenuity?"

"That's it, Charles. That's got to be it. They can't get any further on their own! They have to figure out how to take us to their planet Charles."

"Okay, Olly, then what can we learn from them?"

"A lot! Charles. The first thing we might learn from them is where we came from. The second is where we are going. The latter wouldn't be a tough one because we already know that humans can't yet live forever. We are delicate, we can be extinct in the blink of an eye. But on the other hand we are probably doing much better than other ancient peoples did. Some of our ancestors didn't even make it to the Stone Age, while others could have equaled us in some technologies.

Our current knowledge is about right. We have evolved to the epitome of life. We invented the computer, the pinnacle of learning, and we've invented the atom bomb, the apex of total destruction. It all depends on what they want, peace or war.

They could also have competition; they might want the atom bomb to get rid of their adversaries on other planets."

"On earth though Olly, if the aces want to stay in an English-speaking country, they must learn our language. Should they be allowed to travel? Can they go on vacation to Florida, California, Hawaii, Europe, Japan, Australia, or Mexico?"

"Sure Charles. They don't have to ask, they will go where they are programmed to go."

I am thinking that Klutch could be faking it, saying he's from Wales. He could be from some planet that has zero gravity where nothing wears out. Klutch could last forever. Maybe he has to be maintained though, every ten thousand years or so. Imagine if you could go to visit aces at their home, and you took a car there, your car would last forever on that planet, but you would die – on the way there, or on the way home. Because we are mortal.

I am trying to walk my fingers up on the side of my right leg. I can only bend my forefinger part way. On the left side it's the same thing. Is this partial paralysis? But I'm not paralyzed, just restrained. I'm in great trouble. I attempt to rotate my head from side to side – even if just 20 to 30 degrees.

It's working, I can move my head from side to side, up and down a little to check on myself. What have I done to be in a situation like this? This is torture. I can't possibly be in a civilized country.

Torture is not allowed in the civilized world. Unless... I've been kidnapped by a communist group known as ISDE (International Social Democracy Everywhere), in that case I'm done for. They are fanatics and will never come to check on me, and I will die. I don't want to die. Not that I don't deserve to. The people that put me here though, can't possibly know or prove any of the bad things I have done in my life. The burning body is back now the rain is coming down a little harder again.

The small patch of water is morphing into a puddle right here where I am sitting and the layer of oil is shimmering on top. That's what I'm afraid of. I am hoping it will stop raining before it gets much deeper.

I don't even know if I'm in a valley or on top of a hill. I might be on flat ground and there's no danger of flooding. But if I am in a low-lying area shaped like a tub... then I'm in big trouble. I could be in a riverbed, but that's not likely because there is no movement in this oily water.

However, the oil is lighter than water and it will stay on top for sure, whether it is moving or not. I must figure out a way to get out of this steel frame. I am an engineer. An engineer's job is to solve problems! Come on Charles! I know I have shoes on, but I can barely see them now. They are covered in water already. I can move my right heel closer to the stone seat and ease it up and down slightly. I am happy about that. I can move my left heel too, but I can't get my feet together. My feet seem to be in different cuffs. If I rub my shoes against the block I'm sitting on, I can wear them down enough to remove them, or maybe I can force them off. They are definitely in separate metal cuffs. I am trying to lick the rain from my lips. My lips always taste like soot, but I can still get some dampness. Now there is at least four inches of water around my shoes.

I thought I heard thunder. If it was thundering it had to be miles away. I start counting the seconds - one second, one mile… I remembered that from grade school. My feet are wet, because my shoes are soaked through. I should start praying, if only I knew how. I should pray for the rain to stop and the lightning not to set the oil on fire. What do people do instead of praying? Wish? Swear? Curse? I can start counting sheep and hope to fall asleep. That's not good. I want to be awake if something happens, if anything will. I see flashes of light, far away. I still hear thunder. I try to lift my shoes off the ground. I can move them, maybe two inches.

My mind is getting numb. It feels like bushels full of zeroes are flowing out of my head again adding to the water at my feet. It feels like I'm surrounded with zeroes and ones, and they are cascading down and away from me. Maybe they will prevent me from burning up if lightning strikes this puddle. What would I do if lightning actually caught the oil on fire? I imagine the fire could envelope the whole area with me in the middle of it. I would fry like bacon in a pan. Except I'm still alive. Fried alive!

Not possible! I'm crying. I don't remember ever crying since I was a child.

I imagine my shoes catching fire and then my pants. I am trying to blow the fire out but can't.

I am trying to move my feet up and down creating a turbulence in the water. Maybe the turbulence would put the fire on my pants out. But what if it doesn't?

Crying is not going to help me. Thank God there is no fire yet. I used to have a little knife in my pant pocket, left pocket? Right? I think I had the pocketknife in my right pocket. I'll see if I can reach it. Keep trying, keep on trying I tell myself. If I could find my knife, I could cut my pant leg off and kick it away before it catches on fire.

How would I transfer my knife into my other hand? How? How? Now the rain is starting up again. I can't feel my knife at all.

There is something there! It is just dirt. If I could bend my hand to reach up, or down. Maybe if I could loosen the chain and feed part of it to my hand, I could go downwards with my fingers into my pocket... no luck. My fingers are not moving any more than three or four inches away from my seat.

The rain is getting stronger. I can see the drops make rings on the surface of the puddle. Don't panic! Just don't panic, I keep telling myself. And what if I do panic? What happens then? I still can't go anywhere. I am licking the rain off my lips and the moisture tastes salty. That means they are mixed with tears! In front of me the fire in this person's gut is not getting any less fierce. I can still hear the whooshing sounds. Something is definitely feeding that fire.

Now we are back on Rest Acres Road. I'm standing beside the Tesla when suddenly I hear Olly questioning me; "Charles, have you ever assassinated anyone in your life?" Olly asks this question out of the blue. My knees became play dough, but I pulled myself together. I just lean onto the car and quickly mull over the word 'assassinate'. This had to be a loaded question. Olly examines the road gravel as he waits for my answer. I know I am not a killer, at least not a killer of any individual per se. I might have killed dozens of combatants with drones or guided missiles but not one particular person or alien. Hope he is not thinking of me as an assassin.

"No Olly, why? Have you got someone in mind?" I asked.

He replies with a Yany, "not now and we don't blot people out for little things. We usually get a *call*. The person is a ruler, a king, a dictator, or a president and the termination is done by elaborate covert ways, of course."

He chuckles as he says this and I'm thinking of Saddam and General Gaddafi.

"Anything can happen in a conflict, Charles, and there are conflicts even in the USA between the two competing political parties, you know that."

"I got you Olly," I said, and breathed a little easier. Here we go, he's pausing too long after talking, and now I'm back on the stone. The burning body is back too and now the rain is coming down a lot harder. Where I sit, the small patch of water under my shoes is growing into a larger puddle and the thin layer of oil is still shimming on top. None of this is any good. I am hoping it will stop raining before the puddle gets much deeper. I can't get the water out of my mind. I certainly don't want to be sitting in water on top of everything else. Even if it doesn't catch on fire, I could still drown. It would have to pour really hard for the water to reach the stone where the body is burning. Never mind the stone where the body is burning! I'll be flooded long before the water reaches that pyre. I listen… nothing. I can't hear anymore noises or cries coming from behind. I can only hear the hissing from the burning body.

The grader starts to pull the loaded water tank truck away from the ditch and proceeds going forward and the annoying beeping noise stops. The flag man motions us to go, and I climb back into the car and fasten my seat belt. Olly too gets in, but he doesn't do up his belt until the bell starts to chime then he only wraps it around his knees. That bothers me. I automatically fasten my belt whenever I sit in a car, whether I'm by myself or chauffer driven. Am I getting paranoid? "Charles, we are getting close to our street that hasn't even been named yet. Just for the heck of it, why don't you give it a shot, come up with a good name for it."

I had never named a street before, why doesn't he name it Olly St. or Olly Alley, it even sounds good? Olly Alley! So, I take it as a challenge and I come up with one in less than twenty seconds.

"*Chief Joseph Parkway*, how does that sound to you Olly? I used to know an artist Dick Jordan, who has painted a lot of famous native personalities including Chief Joseph."

"Hey, Charles, that's a good one."

Olly loved the name and gave me a broad Yany.

"Charles you're a genius, I think that is fabulous, and it is the right name."

I didn't know if Olly had ever heard of Chief Joseph or not, but he might have. I didn't question him. But I enjoyed his approval, he made my day.

"Native people should be paramount in Canada, in fact all of North America, for that matter," I declared.

Olly nodded and said, "sure thing." The seatbelt alert started to chime again, and Olly buckled in this time.

I'm thinking… really now, there are no cops on this Parkway.

I am already calling the road Chief Joseph Parkway, in my mind. So, if there are no cops on this road but he still puts the seat belt on, means he is human. God sure as heck wouldn't have put the belt on. Or if he is God, is this just a ruse?

That's possible too because I still don't really know him.

"In a few minutes Charles, we will be entering 'The Remote Security Zone' RSZ. That's what our plant area is called. It has to be restricted because of the nature of our business. We are dealing with explosives, and we don't want anybody with nefarious ideas to come in here. As you can see, there is no gate or barrier only a sign that says, 'Beyond this point entrance by invitation only'. If a person walking by and wants to enter anyway, he or she is greeted by an aerial robot and instructed to stop and go back. They will be advised by a loudspeaker and if they are in a car and want to keep ongoing the vehicle is disabled. I mean they can't go another foot farther."

"Okay, Olly, but what happens if it is a person on foot and bent on coming in?"

"Well Charles, then an aerial vehicle comes out immediately and tells them the infraction.

Now if the person insists, the police is called and he or she is tasered and removed, of course."

I acknowledged what he said and started thinking, what a good idea.

"We can't have people coming here parading or protesting about this or that, right?" Olly said and continued; "when an unauthorized vehicle attempts to enter, it will lose power immediately. Beyond the imaginary line telephones and all other electronic devices become scrambled, dysfunctional. You're close enough, go ahead see if you can use your phone."

I stopped and turned on my new smartphone and by golly, Olly was right. My phone was scrambled. Olly smiled and told me that he'll get me a *good* one.

"Our devices are special, built to order. This plant is close to the Brantford Airport and this entire air space is under an 'Iron Dome', same as in the United States. Just like them, we cannot be attacked by robots or missiles. This is all done by stationary satellites or 'watcher' satellites. The second someone is firing a hostile intercontinental missile from somewhere in our direction, it explodes in the air, more often in their faces. The US doesn't care much about the millions of soldiers in intimidating armies all over the world. They know conflicts are not hand to hand any more. Armies of any size can be wiped out as easily as an army of one soldier. You know that, Charles. Any other major country like Russia or Germany has Watcher satellites and that's enough. The trick is to have a Watcher satellite in the proximity of the aggressor. If that is not possible…well, then it is up to the space force to deal with them. As you know, world wars are not simple anymore. Come to think of it, I wouldn't want to start one. You've heard about Area 51 or R4808N, which is the USA's official description. Our area is called Area 62. I was happy to hear that. I even asked if the 'dome' was the same as the one in Israel.

"In a way it is, except in the USA it is a lot more sophisticated. The system in Israel is no dog, mind you." Olly remarked assuredly.

I nodded and smiled. I thought that was good to know because you don't want to see a manufacturing plants like this blown up, even if it is in Canada. At least not after it took four years and billions of dollars to build and equip.

*****

As we reached the restricted zone Olly asked me to stop. I stopped and stepped out of the car. I walked around it and walked back and forth and felt nothing. Olly stayed in the car and watched me reading the small print on the sign. There was an email address and a phone number one could call. I didn't memorize it, but I told Olly I didn't feel anything different when I walked across the imaginary line.

He gave me another Yany and said, "I was already inducted."

CHAPTER FOUR

I pulled into a parking spot along the bare wall in front of us. The building had vertical sheet metal siding all around it. This surprised me because generally there's a brick or stone office in the front of a factory. Some of them even have shrubs, plants, or blooming flowers. Here was nothing, just a dozen or so parking spots marked out on the blacktop. The factory looked as if it was unfinished. I hesitated a few seconds because I didn't know which spot to take. This was so unusual to me that I almost asked Olly if he forgot to build the office. I didn't want to sound sarcastic, but I had to ask something that fit this extra ordinary situation.

"Hey Olly, if you invite somebody to this place how do they know where to go?" I asked him completely befuddled. I couldn't have possibly been the first person who ever came visiting here. There's got to be more to this place than meets the eye. On the other hand he might have something up his sleeves, just like in everything else he does. It's always unique and unusual and might even be unprecedented.

"I know what you are thinking Charles. You have stopped at the right place as this is our private entrance, even though you can't see a door. I did it this way just to further discourage people from coming here. As you'll see we have an automatic sliding door that opens to let us in." I was astonished because this was so unreal. A six-foot section of the vertical wall slid upwards, and a door appeared.

"When we have visitors, we do the real thing, sixty feet of the metal from the corner of the building slides away on this end and 100 feet from the front moves to the side. In fact, I am going to show you how it is done right now."

Olly must have pushed a button in his pocket or grimaced at some spot on the building because the front structure began to transform into a fabulous wonderland similar to the Bellagio in Las Vegas, less the piglets, of course. I stood there in total awe. The change happened in about sixty seconds or even less. There were plants shrubs and flowers all natural, natural looking anyway, almost like in a botanical garden.

We went to the front and entered the building through a glass door. A pleasant 'female' receptionist greeted us, (a robot). There was a huge oval screen stretching across the entire room. Olly depressed another button or perhaps it was automatic, and a futuristic Planet-port with space vehicles appeared, and was expanding in size, moving ever so slowly. I don't know where the video was taken. I think it must have been a video in California or Florida or at some other planet, maybe it wasn't real. The scenery to me gave the impression that we were on higher ground – looking down onto something that was happening or had happened at a different time. I gazed at the miraculous landscape in total awe. Just as I was going to comment on this incredible site, Olly touched my arm and nudged me to the left into a brightly lit hall. He led me to an area that at first looked like an empty space but as it became fully illuminated, a huge globe of Earth appeared in front of me. To my left there was an imaginary 'wall of athletes' with an array of famous past and present day basketball, baseball, football and tennis players. They were at eye level just like in real life. They weren't pictures but appeared to be smiling – life like people. In other rows there were celebrities Lady Ga Ga, Beyoncé, Bruce Willis... I felt like greeting them all but then I figured they could not possibly be real. Good thing I didn't address them because Olly would have thought I was talking to myself. I quickly decided to remain silent. Of course, they weren't real and Olly would have thought I had gone crazy. The scenery changed all by itself again as we advanced into this large hall.

"Charles, you are with me now, but in the future, you will be able to find your way to my office on your own as well as to your office which is next to mine. Klutch's area is over a little way past ours. We are at his office right now. He is away on assignment."

Olly had stopped for a moment as if he had forgotten what he was going to say. I wondered how the employees got inside the plant. I was curious because I didn't even see another parking lot. Then I remembered that he said he had no employees in the plant. He must have thought I'd be asking something to that effect, and he was right. I needed to know how people went in and out of this place. He restated the plant ran by itself. Service personnel, when needed would come through subways that connected to the downtown, to the airport and other important locations. He showed me the spacious elevator that could easily transport groups of people, probably machinery too. I nodded my head and kept nodding subconsciously like a bobbing head until I finally digested all he had said and what all I had seen.

*****

I was surfing the computer when Olly came in my office. He had a wide Yany on his face. "Charles, I hope I'm not interrupting something terribly important?"

"My God you sure have some capacity on this baby, don't you?" I declared.

"We have Charles. You don't want a Mickey Mouse for serious work. We just got something added yesterday. We are doing business with various companies in different countries. I am sure you're going to like your job a lot. He opened a door on the opposite wall and beckoned me over. I looked inside and saw a maze of wires tubes shelves switchboards and various computer equipment, Olly wasn't kidding.

"You see, our government wants to start communicating with the extraterrestrials using the English language.

The ones we have here speak very good English already but amongst themselves they use some kind of visage that we don't yet comprehend. They might even be using radio waves. He stopped for a moment and showed me a large Yany.

"An important question arises Charles. If we do business with them, how are they going to pay us? What are they going to pay us with? What are we going to use for money, or in place of money?

Another thing we have to understand, as you know they don't have human cerebrum, they have chips for brains. And chips are machines pre-programmed by superiors, or higher-ranking bosses or 'gods' that look like us and could already be living here, but we don't know who they are.

They stay out of our way and often use motions or eye movements that mean something to them. They can translate these into commands. You know about 'commands'. The government knows who these aliens are, but ordinary people don't, and the common person doesn't care. I believe this because I am compelled to use human thinking and of course we are all human. Right, Charles?" He looked at me with a drawn-out wide Yany.

"We are using human thinking because we are here on earth and not out there in space." I said.

"If you're just 'surfing' the beast (he meant the computer) come on over." Olly said to me as he headed toward his office. I followed him. He sat down in *his* easy chair, and I sat on the sofa opposite side of an enormous coffee table that was big enough for a dancing parquet. He asked me if I had any thoughts about interplanetary communication. I told him I had stationary satellites in mind for data transition. "That too…" Olly said and nodded then went on; "See Charles, if we want to do business with '*them*', what kind of money are we going to use for currency?"

"That's a very interesting question Olly." I said and added "here on earth we use monetary units such as Dollars or Euros. The universe should use something unique like Euros, right?" I asked Olly and spelt 'Euros'.

Olly was licking his lips absent mindedly.

I went on, "the Euros came first so Europe deserves that moniker. Give me another ten seconds to see if I can come up with something more befitting." I chuckled because I had an idea already and when he said 'I dare you' I was ready; "How's about Nebulas. How does Nebulas sound to you, Olly?"

Olly almost stopped breathing. "Bingo, that's perfect! Good name for hard cash Charles."

I felt pretty proud of myself and punched air with my right hand. Especially after he said 'hard cash' because that is exactly what I had in mind. He couldn't have been too far off the mark when he said we were cyber twins. His cellphone dinged, and he answered it. I got up and went back to my office.

*****

I was getting pretty excited, even though most of the otherworldly things I have ever seen and that we have talked about, were assumptions. And often in our conversation we automatically gave the aliens human traits. They had to be using one hell of a computerized system and it was instantaneous too. They had to give the right answer in a particular situation and that was a big job. To take a spoken word in English, process it, then convert it to their language and return the correct answer in English exactly where they had predicted it would fit. It is an almost impossible task. Untold scenarios with an untold number of answers to a situation. That is one hell of a way to speak the language. Maybe, just maybe, that's why they're not getting rid of us just yet, I thought. They could take over *our* world in a blink of an eye if they wanted to. They'd like to take us home, but they know we cannot yet survive inter-planetary travel because we have to eat, drink, eliminate and sleep and not only that, but do they have breathable air on their planet? So, for their experimentations they have to study us here on Earth. But still the question comes up should we agree to all of that? They can combine machines with humans.

Maybe that's why we don't mind having them here because we think we can combine humans with machines. Olly finished his phone and came over and asked me back to his place.

"Nebulas, what a great idea, Charles."

I noticed something in Olly's speech. I don't know what it was, he had that faraway look in his eyes when he said; what a great idea.

"I say this Olly, they don't seem to be interested in our oxygen or any of our manufactured energy, what in hell is it they want then? My guess is they want to relearn our human traits that they must have possessed at one time. You know, over thousands or perhaps millions of years, even light years they could have lost the art of creative thinking and now they can only use robot reasoning."

"This is what I think Charles, they really want to do 'something' with us. They came back to see if we have evolved far enough, to the point they want us to be. I think the time is ripe now. The last time they were here maybe twenty or thirty thousand years ago, we weren't ready. Oh, by the way, we configure time in hours and days and years, they could be counting in light years."

"You think so, Olly?" I asked hesitantly. I was worrying about his state of mind.

"Thirty thousand years ago, Charles I don't know how many years it is to them, but I don't think our intelligentsia was developed well enough yet. If they want to learn something from us, the time is now, whatever time it is to them. Think about it Charles, we have invented the world's most powerful teaching machine, the computer, and the world's most destructive device the nuclear bomb. I don't know which one they are looking for, maybe both or neither. All I know is they are a lot more advanced than we are. What I would like to know is how many different aliens are out there or are they all from the same planet? Our government has to answer that question.

I sure as hack wouldn't want different aliens competing for us here on earth. Whether there are other more desirable ones out there I don't know. What *they* want from us is the question. Do they want us to help them, or do they want us to help them destroy their competition, what do you think Charles?"

He had this strange look in his eyes and now he spoke with an unsteady voice; "You'll have to hold the fort for a couple days, Charles, I have to go to a special meeting. Special! Cocos Island, you know where that island is?"

I didn't know where it was, and Olly told me that he'll fly in with a helicopter from someone's yacht. This sounded like something really special. But I told him not to worry I'd be here.

*****

I wondered what this was all about. Maybe he had to eliminate someone, start a war somewhere, I'll just have to wait. Olly said if he had to make a choice between several aliens he wouldn't know which aliens we'd want here on earth either. We'd have to see if we had a choice. Then he said; "Yeah, Charles whatever *human* brain they once had – it is lost. They must have some highly developed system though, don't you think?" He asked me.

"Yeah, I read you, Olly. They must have brains – or some substance stuffed into a head or wherever, some kind of *living plastic* yet unknown to us. Here on earth hey get away with fake mouths, noses and ears and eyes on their heads but not necessarily or exactly in front of their faces. No one is criticizing them for that. You can tell, if one's looking close enough, their eyes aren't focused on what they are gazing at. They try to look exactly like us in the worst way, and some of them almost do Olly." I said and thought of things I can get done while he was away. He excused himself and sat down by his computer and started to look up Cocos Island. I waved to him as I moseyed out of his office.

*****

My mind was jerked back to the blackened stone. My state of mind couldn't decide where I should be. I was in and out the story I carried on with Olly and the burning body is in front of me. Then I had to think really hard to figure out what happened to me. Did somebody do something to me where was I what was it, where did they take me? How did I even get there? I may not even be in Canada now. I must have said something about killing someone with an armored drone. Or did my torturers accuse me of killing somebody of their own? My mind is erratic, I see other strange people around me... they are shackling me, taking me outside, I am calling for Olly... they are sticking a needle in my arm...

*****

Olly is back home from Cocos Island and I'm in his office sitting on the couch and he is in his easy chair opposite from me.

He is anxious. Hesitating, I can't understand his behavior… it seems like he is about to tell me something. He is clearing his throat.

"Charles, this is a big thing, but before I tell you… you have to promise me you won't say anything about this until it is officially announced. I mean to no one, not even your family."

"Ok Olly, I won't." I answer quickly.

His hair is messed up he looks wild. He stops talking and stares at me with piercing eyes. I have never seen him like this. He carries on, "I, and now you Charles, belong to a Special Segment of Society. (SSS)." He says this while moving closer to the edge of his easy chair.

"Are you kidding me Olly?" I ask and slide a bit closer to the edge of the couch too, almost falling off.

"Charles, this is not a joke, and this will blow your mind, guaranteed. Just listen to me." Olly says this as he moves back in his chair.

"The society we belong to has established contact with the 'high command' on planet E28. A line of communication has been created and their language has been deciphered. A very important person from the US is already there, and the news is great. I mean fantastic, out of this world, literally. Now that you are one of us you too should be aware of what the society has in mind. As you know there are a lot of millionaires and billionaires in the world Charles, this is what's coming down the pipes but won't be announced for a while.

This won't be in the newspapers for some time. This concerns us millionaires only. That of course includes you too Charles."

Olly paused and with piercing eyes looked 'through me' and said very seriously, "starting next year we'll be the first ones to travel to and reside on planet E28. We have seen videos of beautiful city scenes, hotels, mansions under construction, streets, highways, airports being built there, and they will greet us when we get there. Remember how we talked about 'humans dying out' on a planet?"

"Yeah Olly, from an earth disease, I remember we talked about that."

"Well that happened on E28 Charles. This is a very important point you have to remember. Once you are a millionaire, it does not matter what country you're from or how many millions you have, you can't take any money with you. You will not need money anymore. Your wealth will be left here on earth and will pay (several times over) for what's needed for ordinary folks to have a worry-free life. It is left on earth to correct all the infrastructures, fulfill hollow promises even in the poorest countries of the world that have been neglected for many years, decades or even centuries. In America what you see happening today is that liberals are miss-leading people, telling them to get rid of capitalism and embrace socialism, Marxism. They will not succeed.

The caveat is planet E28. There are no politics or *race*, no black or white or yellow or red, everyone will be the same color – sun-tanned. Children don't know the difference between races, and they don't care about the different languages either, they will understand each other immediately. Adults will speak the language they learned at home. But when their Mega Chip (MC) kicks in they will default to Enhanced Intelligence (EI). Everyone will understand each other. How about that, Charles?"

"Awesome, wow." I said and started thinking.

"Beginning this year, we millionaires and our friends, relatives with at least one million dollars will be admitted to planet E28 and reside there with their families. On E28 no one is privileged because everyone is 'special'. Nefarious thoughts such as hate and hostility are removed from the chips only passion and love allowed.

From the wealth left on earth, the USA, will start printing enough money to begin converting even the most deprived people's lives into nations of comfort, happiness, caring and enjoyment."

I closed my mouth and stopped blinking. I almost stopped inhaling too.

"I'm telling you this Charles, there will be special robots designated for earth and different ones for those on planet E28."

"What do you mean by 'different' Olly?"

"There's a lot of difference Charles. The biggest difference is that we (the ones who qualified with our wealth) have done our job on earth either through our talents, brains, ambition, ingenuity, or inheritance. Let's face it Charles, we are different from ordinary folk. We, 'capitalist millionaires' on our future planet E28, will have what we always wanted. Modern structures, homes, cars, boats, planes everything for our enjoyment.

For restoring humanity on E28, everything is a gift to us. E28 robots will do all the chores imaginable, and they'll do those automatically so that their makers can flourish and advance further, perhaps become leaders in the whole universe. This is a new era on planet E28 and certainly in our lives.

We have found what we always wanted – a place for unlimited opportunities to create and pursue even higher living standards with our 'mechanical' comrades in beautiful cities, luxurious houses where every chore is done with Robot Caretakers (RC-s).

These <u>Robot Caretakers are especially designed for serving humans on planet E28. These robots are 100% 'self-aware', just like human beings!</u>

This is not new to the robots Charles. Many, many centuries ago they were created and indoctrinated to do every job assigned to them. They don't ask questions; they don't complain and they never criticize anything. They have been programmed to observe, diagnose, and follow instructions to a T. Their normal stature and appearance are exactly like ours. They are beautiful or handsome.

The perfect kind of robots for humans!

For our transportation to E28, spacious shuttle vehicles have been designed and are in mass production there right now.

On earth, Charles, there'll be Helper Robot aces, (HR) *robots* for all disciplines. These robot aces too are 'self-aware'. They'll assist in all endeavors, tasks, or chores, they will even assist in choosing one's facial and bodily appearance, even the color of one's skin. Preferred color will be 'sun-tanned'. Seemingly a big job, but not really, everything is done by computer in living color. Just imagine Charles, you stand in the front of a mirror and look at yourselves in living color. People who are not used to computers will be taught through a chip and will become acquainted with the technology and all the normal life expectancies or experiences that they will use every day. People will be guided by special, highly trained concierges who will teach everyone and will *handle* any situation – very efficiently.

At the beginning these phenomenal HR aces are sun-tanned in appearance, like everyone else but they'll flash blue when they are on the move, accomplishing a service and will emit a beeping sound when backing up; similar to service vehicles today. At the beginning many of them will be vandalized shot and assaulted. But when that happens, they will crumble into heaps (defensive mode, DM) and disappear even at the slightest aggression against them, leaving the antagonist befuddled. DM procedure will be demonstrated in all cities of the world to everyone in their own language and will be common everywhere.

There will be a video of the DM procedure on everyone's IPod, so that humans won't be surprised, they will know what is going on. These numerous humanlike HR aces will keep to themselves and be courteous in their manner. They won't eat drink or defecate they will stand aside or stay in the designated shelters of their human superiors and will assist families or individuals as desired. Every human of any race, creed or religion will have a home (comfortable residences will be in abundance) everyone will have 'their castle'. There won't be drug overdoses because the 'killer' drugs will be identified and removed. There will be no drug dealers! Intoxication by alcohol or by any other means will be rare and inconvenient, very easily monitored or avoided completely.

Migrants will be called travelers, tourists going to places they want to see, or even to live there.

Courts, or jails won't be needed.

At the beginning, sanatoriums will be provided for those people who require a cure.

Instead of police there will be 'Security Service Personnel' (SSP aces). SSP aces understanding every imaginable discipline. At the start mental deficiencies will be diagnosed and corrected on the chip and cured!

Everyone, including all indigenous people everywhere will become happy in their own skin and their environment, practicing their religion or beliefs in their community. Those that felt misunderstood who felt lonely and abandoned will be re-chipped will be enlightened and happy and receive guidance from HR aces, or SSP ace professionals for as long as required. Wars, violence, cyberwars will be eliminated. Fake representation, fake news will be corrected. Chips, Mega-chips, re-chipping are verbal expressions, you will hear often. Newborn babies will have Life-Guard chip in their bodies that will prevent them from all known human diseases.

Manners and behaviors, actions and reactions, feelings, compassions, love, are the same as we already know them, but some will be tweaked, adjusted to common standards. Desire to kill another human being will be wiped out completely.

At the beginning vandalism against robots by humans will be numerous but will be senseless and eradicated completely.

Natural, superior talent in any discipline, will be compared to a mega chip and will be recognized, deciphered, and rewarded by E28 status and given a chance to transfer to that planet on demand.

Life on earth will reach E28 level pretty quickly in 15, 20 years, however restoration of the environment will take a lot longer.

While tornados, hurricanes, tsunamis, and other climatic disasters such as earthquakes and volcanoes are tamed, some will remain. Better building practices will help. The greatest reward will be 'the E28 Prize', just like the Nobel Prize except more numerous and incentivized and highly revered. Re-chipping will be a simple procedure, done locally and completed to the recipient's <u>desired</u> degree.

For future inhabitants, on E28, even childbirth will be done by robots you need only to inseminate the female person you love and the rest will be through robot, 'robot mothers' unless otherwise desired. Abortion on E28 and on earth will be eliminated. Will never be needed because the health and sex of the fetus is always a given, pre-arranged between partners and created on demand. Then it is automatically analyzed, screened and processed. How many children you want is your choice?

You and your partner decide whether you want a child or children created. It is not important to have more children for prosperity's sake. Rape is scrubbed from all chips.

On planet E28 and on earth there is no longer a need to categorize any group or race of people because they all are special, all belong here and will live to enjoy their 'identity'. Everyone is special. This is a wonderful feeling that everyone will have everywhere.

The desire to be a president of planet E28 is totally irrelevant. It is a chore and is handled very efficiently by robot hierarchy.

Since there is no politics to worry about on E28 (remember, there's no money on planet E28) it runs itself through autonomous 'Expert Life Guides' (ELG-s). This society was created eons –ago but the 'original humans' have died out due to earthly diseases.

Current and future epidemics will be monitored and eventually cured as they come along.

Common Life Guides (CLG-s) on earth will appear the moment they are needed. No one among earth-dwellers will have the notion to kill anyone, not even out of jealousy. 'Mental deficiency' eradicated! This and other negative traits are not installed into Mega Chips. If you want spousal change, it will be a given, as easy as changing your shirt, only minor revision in one's chip is required. Accidents may happen but will be quickly reverted, defaulting to normal, to what it was before. In most cases it will be averted or avoided. There will be Angel Robots (AR's) and Watcher Robots (WR's) to guide you and your mode of transportation. Whether it is on E28, whether it is on earth your trip is mapped out for your convenience as we trot along. Nefarious thoughts aren't put on chips. Professional guidance will be available to everyone in the instance that it is required.

On earth guidelines are not yet 'written in stone' but number one preference will be given to changing people's behaviors to meet E28 standards. Robots on earth and on E28 are crafted with 'self-awareness'. Free robot service, when required, is available to every person over the age of twenty years and older if or when called for.

Robots don't need food, water, or special care. They however will disappear upon any violence towards them!

It has been ascertained that earth was living on its 'last leg'.

Planet E28 has been created for millionaires and – acclimatized and designed just like earth and has become available to earth dwellers and is free of pollution. Due to uncorrectable and fatal sequences in nuclear reactions, life on earth will have ended in 100-150 years. On earth, poisoning the seas, oceans with micro-plastics and over fertilizing the land reached a point of no return. Emergence of Covid-19 like diseases slowly but reluctantly would have decimated all the people. Animal life will have struggled but survived. Political decisions will have collapsed and gotten to a point where even the creators themselves would have gone crazy trying to follow them.

On earth, after robots were given the job of 'heavy lifting' people started enjoying everything, learning different languages, and travelling to places where they always wanted to go. Anyone could go visiting other more remote planets, even to the ones without any human life, like planet E26, with earthlike weather, wildlife, oceans, and lakes, but uninhabitable for humans because of too much carbon dioxide. This condition will be corrected in the next few decades or so to accept earth's inhabitants who eventually want to transfer there. Giving earth another chance to replenish.

From planet E28 anyone will be able to travel back to earth just to see how the 'ordinary' people have gotten along.

Space travel may need some easily achievable adjustment – usually concerning weight and volume.

To those people who wanted to return to live on earth it is possible, homesickness is common. This happens often – not a big thing. They will be using special UFOs accept they'll be called (IFO's; Identified Flying Objects), or USO-s (Underwater Submersible Objects). One may want to go back to earth, to work hard or think hard or to start all over – until becoming a millionaire again and re-qualifying for E28 status. Some people may do that (just to prove a point). Some may get bored with life all together and pack it in. Saying 'two lifetimes is enough'.

On earth priests and religious leaders who are driven by their beliefs or faith will remain put and practice unabridged. Their flock will endure. Preventative watcher robot aces will stop uprisings, riots homicides and suicides. Those who attempt to form illegitimate governments, so called power grabbers spreaders of 'untruths' are soon recognized and discouraged, if they insist, prohibited from ever entering planet E28 altogether. (They can be re-chipped on demand). Professionals will teach humanity in schools where students will clearly learn 'The International Constitution' (TIC) law.

Indigenous millionaires and 'family' – will also go to E28. They can themselves decide who to take along. Those who remain on earth will have access to watcher robot aces to help them in any circumstance.

Fake news will be canceled instantly, shot down or corrected by watcher robot ace editors, (AE-s). Politics on earth that were once ingrained in certain humans for all the wrong reasons will change to traits or fashions. Hundreds of thousands will be free of deranged politics like Fascism or Communism.

On earth, bright leaders, ambitious organizers, inventers, innovators, and scholars – writers, poets, artists and composers will be celebrated and appreciated. They will be proud of their achievements and become new candidates to E28. A big thing it is and will be.

On planet E28 houses, mansions, haciendas will be built and run by capable pleasant robot ace caretakers. Your clothes – the most beautiful, fashionable created by robot seamstresses, even your shoes ties, gowns, cars, yachts, planes made especially for you as you desire. Vehicles will be piloted or driven by professional robot personnel or auto piloted or by yourself, as you desire. All jobs even the 'most menial' or the 'most intricate' will be done by robot aces.

For seniors on E28 here's the kicker, you may go back to live in the best years of your life, you can revert to the 'best years of your life Charles. Can you fathom that?"

"I couldn't." I said and continued my amazement.

"The life you always wanted and pined for and as long as you desire to have it. You may go into suspended life mode for a day, a year or two, or for a decade or forever. It is as you wish. You can even die – we will miss you. You're allowed to die. This happens when you get bored, too much of perfect life can become boring.

Even to have the best of everything can be overbearing, too much on E28.

On earth you don't have to do anything you don't want to do. You may start a business, a sport, collecting, mountain climbing or anything just for a while and you don't yet know for how long. You don't yet know where you belong or what was cut out for you in your life. An easily reachable number you can call 'lifeline' (LL), and they will help you choose a direction for you. Then you're given an expert robot ace counselor. You may carry on or start something else until you shake into the right groove. You might want to be a leader, a president of a company, a chief, a chef or a tradesman or a crafter in any line you feel comfortable. Or you can wait until you decide to do something great. (Your robot ace counselor will give you options, the counselor will see what you're best suited for)!

Now Charles, what do you think?"

I soiled my pants.

CHAPTER FIVE

"We are going to be schooled and taught how to communicate with our alien robots Charles."

So, this is why Olly went to Cocos Island, I thought. Surely a fantastic gift from E28 aces. I couldn't fall asleep for days. I can't fall asleep anyway now because I'm still shackled to this stone! As long as my mind is busy imagining fabulous places in other worlds, it is devoid of my misery.

I am in Olly's office now and Olly is talking about all the places we can travel to in the future. He continues, "when we conduct business with robots our behavior will come automatically. One thing for certain Charles, the robots will not allow any aggressive conduct against them. They'll revert to DM, (defensive mode). They'll crumble and disappear."

All I could say was wow.

"Just a couple more things Charles, have you ever seen aliens with children?"

"Come to think of it Olly, I guess I haven't."

"When children are needed Charles, or when adult aliens need to be with children, they'll request robots that are made to look like kids and act like kids. These children... of course will never grow up. They are created for showcasing only. They even talk like regular kids, but it's all just to suit the occasion.

There will be aliens in different countries that are specially chipped and re-sized. There'll be thousands of them on earth, millions, to accommodate every age. On earth they will be 'sun-tanned' to avoid conflicting with different 'races'.

The gender of the robots is uniform, they are sexless drones Charles. They are programmed to remember where *they have been!* And they *do* remember where they have been, because sometimes they have to go back to that same location. For safety reasons they change their bases often and they don't reside for too long in one area. They cannot be kidnapped, shot, drowned, hurt or killed in any way. If they are assaulted, they crumble into a heap, then disappear. Leaving the perpetrator befuddled. This goes for all aliens Charles. When they are surprised or violated, they are programmed to disappear. This comes automatically to them. They are complicated machines, and they will not remain in an accident or at a crime scene in pieces. They simply vanish."

I swallowed and kept thinking… could Olly be one of them?

I had to think really hard to remember everything he said.

*****

To change the subject, I asked Olly if he knew what the aliens did with our cannabis derivatives. Our government used to be tightlipped about all alien business. But I went ahead with my question anyway because it could still be relevant.

"Did you see the headlines in the Ideas & Discoveries magazine, *Cannabis - nature's success story? Today there are at least 113 useful cannabinoid compounds that have potential as medically active substances."* I asked Olly.

"No, I didn't, Charles. I missed that one. They probably use them on some 'E' planet he replied."

I said, "it is too bad, because it was a very important discovery when it all happened in China about 6000 years ago. The world has been using hemp or cannabis ever since.

The research station in Simcoe, Norfolk County picked it up and wanted to use it as a replacement crop for tobacco. By the way that's the town I'm from Olly."

"Right on." Olly said.

"Yeah Olly, it was under the headline 'What Conditions Can cannabis heal?' And it was formulated about forty years ago."

"It sounds alien to me too Charles."

I carried on, "the research has been taken over by the Western University in London, Ontario. Back then they called it the *The Wonders of Cannabis*. It is a widely used commodity in complex medical activities all over the world. We can make jelly and jams and soft drinks and cosmetics with it as well. Wonder what the extraterrestrials would do with cosmetics?" I chuckled.

Then I said to Olly, "in small quantities cannabis is actually good for you. Every part has nutrition in it even the seed."

Olly faked amazement but I think he was just ready to look up something on the internet. I must have triggered his mind when I mentioned a *plant*. He could have been thinking of some *other plants* like poppy – for making *heroin*. I stayed in his office for a while and watched him zero in on *'poppy'* seeds.

I thought of my buddy, Adrien whose complete knowledge of 'Growing Cannabis' should have become a legend in Norfolk County. But my story would have taken up quite a bit of time and it was probably irrelevant to Olly, anyway. For some reason he was more interested in cultivating poppies.

Adrian has passed on now, but I think about him a lot. Before he started smoking pot, he used to be a *two pack a day cigarette* smoker and he quit *cold turkey* he said. That part didn't stir too much excitement in me because I did the same thing when I quit smoking decades ago, except I didn't start smoking pot. However I listened when he described the perilous mechanics of growing cannabis. I couldn't even imagine what prompted a farmer to mingle in this 'serious scientific territory'. Farmers had their job cut out when they decided to growing cannabis.

*****

When Olly was done on his computer, he came over to my office and ended my reminiscing about Adrien.

"Come to think of it, I too should have noticed that article Charles", he said.

"I remember Charles, reading about the *tasteless, odorless white powder* that could be added to almost anything, including cosmetics. Maybe our robots want to dazzle some other earthlike planetarians with *our* cosmetics." Olly said matter of factly.

Then he said, "did you know some robots from some planets can travel anywhere by thought Charles. They can go to wherever they want to go. Their thoughts would take them there. By 'thought' they can be here today and billions of miles away tomorrow. They might know some other planets where they can use our cannabis derivative for something vitally important. We cannot travel by thought yet and I don't think we will soon either. Just imagine, Charles, once the WHOLE universe is mapped, we can say, *I want to go to XYZ planet* and the next thing you know you're there. We wouldn't have to worry about speed, eating, drinking, eliminating, or sleeping. Can you imagine travelling like that, to planet XYZ Charles?"

"Beats travelling by car," I said and "beats walking" I added, and went on, "beats doing anything, almost like buying from Amazon, if you don't like the product just send it back and it's gone. Or just tell them 'they sent the wrong thing'. They'll say, 'just keep it' and they'll send you the one you 'ordered'. We don't

80

even have to move our bodies anymore; we only have to use our brains (part of our brains) and our fingertips." I said.

"You are dead on", Olly said and continued; "We too will become machines – that is our future. Is that what we want? Is that what will become of us?"

Olly looked at my nose, my right ear, my hair – probably thinking of me as the final real human being he'll ever see.

*****

"We have testing grounds for aerial drones Charles, testing the most recent drones that the world has not yet seen. We can test spaceships too, however we have to fly them around in *our* Universe. We have a tough time with speed, you know. When we're testing drones, we still have to wear these 'clunky' glasses, but our engineers are working on much lighter ones and they will be available soon. Through these glasses you can appreciate speed and space.

Here on earth, we are still stuck with Einstein's theory 'but the sky's the limit'. In space there is no limit that we know of. With thought, the aliens can go anywhere, or do anything imaginable. I think that's the way it works. You match the atmosphere, speed and gravitation wherever you go." Olly said and went on, "some extraterrestrials from who knows where, come visiting us and don't realize they are in *our* Universe, and we have *gravity*. They should know better, here they have to deal with gravity. They should be able to slow down to any speed," Olly said as we moved to another area in the hallway, the scenery automatically changed to a pristine countryside.

"As you can see Charles, they are finishing the tunnels and installing the vacuum tubes. We are going to be connected to the IVACS (International Vacuum System). When they are finished, we can travel anywhere in the country, if you can afford it. It is still cheaper than air travel and a heck of a lot faster. The only trouble is, it is only for a limited quantity of persons at a time. In a vacuum you don't have to worry about gravity, but it is far from the way the aliens travel, they go via thought, light years converted to thoughts. On earth IVACS is handy for heads of governments as they can meet daily if they want to."

We went out into a large hall and trough a concealed door to the testing 'grounds'.

Olly continued; "here on earth we use holograms for research and sometimes we have objects to move around. You can actually touch our holograms, sort of. Dennis Gabor the inventor of the hologram would turn in his grave if he could see how much his technology has advanced over the last fifty years."

After I put my three 'D' glasses on, I was enthralled with the view of a section of countryside with a lake that materialized before my eyes. Olly put on a set too and switched to my channel.

"We can add boats in a lake as required. Have you ever worked with holograms?" Olly asked.

"A little, but basically no." I said.

I looked at the landscape behind him. The effect of the hologram that radiated through Olly made him bug eyed and his body looked contorted. It appeared as though we were in another world. I had to tell him the truth – other than what I read in books and what I saw on TV I had zero experience with holograms or AR, Augmented Reality either.

"Looking through these glasses Olly, do I look normal to you?" I asked.

"No, Charles. The hologram still plays tricks on anything that is alive. Technology is getting better all the time and one day someone will perfect it. You can actually feel the outline of some objects by hand. I'm sure you will like this and will figure it out for yourself, Charles. You can experiment here and see everything you want and instantly, in real time. I am going to bring up the Oval Office in the White House. You might be able to see people going in and out there," he laughed.

I was astonished. He took me through the famous (infamous) Blue Room, then out into the Rose Garden. A thought occurred to me, just to make him work and to prove it to me – I asked him to reveal the casino where we had a sandwich the other day. Could he ever! He even brought up the room we had been in. This is really handy, I thought. I could use locations in my programming, and they would be totally accurate in every aspect.

"This is absolutely unbelievable, Olly," I said and waited for a Yany.

Olly gave me a half grimace and I guess he didn't want to waste a complete Yany on me at this time.

"I'll show you how to operate the virtual buttons, Charles. It's not hard. Everything is similar to your computer, and you can bookmark things that way too. This is a 'hands on' operation without hands, get it?"

"I got it" I said.

Olly showed me a keyboard in an empty space and how to navigate it with my thoughts. Then he left me alone, and I practiced with it for a while. This was as easy as child's play. I brought up my birthplace and the area where I grew up. I found the hillside by my grandparent's place where the Russians and the Germans fought during the war and where Paul, my uncle and I buried dead soldiers. I saw my schools, my soccer field, my house, until I tired.

I could rotate a building to see more of the surrounding landscape, where the burned wheat field was, and then I went inside the house where my grandparents lived which too was awesome. Everything came up lifelike. This is going to be easy and a heck of a lot of fun. It was certainly a lot easier than I thought it would be. I could think up scenarios. If I needed to, I could play them out and check them and double check them. If my idea didn't work, I could just start over.

As I looked away from the screen, I was suddenly back on the stone and I saw a flash of light to the left of the burning body. It had to be lightning.

I automatically started counting. One, two, three, four, five, six, seven, eight, nine and I hear faint thunder. It was nine miles away. In a way, it is better to be sitting in the rain rather than sitting on this stone in bright sunlight and sweating with the temperature at forty degrees centigrade. If it is daytime now, which I think it is, but I really have no idea about the time; I can figure out if the storm is coming or going by just counting after each flash. Seven! The storm is coming this way. Well, the storm is coming should I worry more? It's not getting any lighter or darker. How long have I been sitting here ... hours? Couldn't have been too long as my legs would be cramping if it was a day or many days. The lightning frightens me though. What if the lightning strikes the accumulated water and sets the oil on fire? What kind of oil is this?

CHAPTER SIX

Olly had told me *this project* was commissioned a few months ago and at that time it didn't appear to be urgent. But suddenly now it's a go.

'Ah hah", he is saying, "just as soon the kids are finished with it, we'll take a look to see what they've come up with. And that's when our work begins".

What is happening to me? Despite the beehive in my head I thought I could stay on top of subjects, things would fall into place. I must have had a conversation with this woman, a fine-looking Jamaican person named Kristina. She is the principal at the Kingston School and she is telling me the curriculum in Jamaica is pretty much the same as it is all over North America. The kids learn science, about the atmosphere, light, sounds and forces that change the earth. They learn about the universe, the sun, the moon, the clouds, and storms.

"We spend a lot of time on computers, information technology stuff (IT), and 3D-4D printers and manufacturing." Kristina said.

I of course, wasn't expecting any high-level computer language like BASIC, C, C++, COBOL, Java, FORTRAN, Ada and Pascal, that the universities teach in Canada and in the United States.

I listened and acknowledged all she said and asked her, "What would you say if I offered money to your students to *'experiment'* three or four hours a week, after regular school hours. From time to time I would give them a *project* and they could figure out what props or tools they might need. The children would be paid in American dollars."

"How much money are we talking about Charles?"

"Twenty-five dollars per hour for each child."

Kristina smacked her lips. "That's a lot of money Charles. Our school needs money. Can we decide how much the children get and keep the rest for our dire needs?"

I realized she was right. I thought it would be best if I just gave her the money and let her decide how to spend it. I told her I'll get a project soon and we'll discuss it together. She was very receptive to that, and I was satisfied when she offered a handshake. Shaking hands with a woman felt very pleasant to me. I haven't been this close to a female for years. It was a good feeling, reinvigorating. But where did I go after that meeting?

It seems to me that Olly must have given me this *project* shortly after I met Kristina. Yes. Sure! Olly had told me to gather information on the different fish that strive in the Rio Grande.

This was a big job. I had to find out what the fish were feeding on in the river and how they multiplied. I had to see if there was any commercial fishing on that river and if there was, who owned the fisheries. Also, I had to find out the existing method of fishing there. The kids had to see what equipment they might need to catch the fish.

"Do you have any idea of what we are after?" Olly asked me.

I replied that had an idea but the exact details I hadn't worked out yet. I said that I had to take another trip to Jamaica and give Kristina the job.

"I think it is obvious," I said to Olly. "The river has all kinds of native fish in it, and we'll have to find a method of raising more of the popular types and perhaps industrialize the operation." I was thinking of nets, of course.

"Very good Charles, but I don't think it's that easy. There has to be something else, and the 'something else' is the kicker." Olly said.

In any case I thought it had a lot to do with catching the fish with nets or by other means and getting the river up to higher fish production. I had to prepare Kristina accordingly.

*****

The plane was going to land in Kingston in a few minutes, the pilot reported. I'm staying at the Pegasus hotel and can hardly wait to jump into the pool or the hot tub. ...But if she is not married... I'm thinking... The plane landed, and I caught a taxi to my hotel. I push Kristina's number on my tablet. She's busy, but her secretary tells me that she will call me back the minute she is free. She says I was number one priority. That's always nice, to be number one.

Thinking about the water in the pool and the hot tub, brought me back to the rainwater and to the blackened stone again but the desire to be with Kristina over ruled my misery.

*****

As I am waiting for Kristina to call, I make myself a drink of vodka and soda water. The brand name on the vodka bottle is Sobieski. That's Polish. What is Polish vodka doing in Jamaica?

I am all alone in this comfortable room and I can do whatever I want. I feel melancholy, a bit lonely. The theme of my room is burgundy, and the window is looking at the Blue Mountain range. I lay down on my bed, which is big enough to accompany a family of four. Above the bed are two pictures of seashells – common in Jamaica, shouldn't even bother to remember them, but I do. I'm thinking of a time when I was married and travelled to Florida with my wife... first wife, second? We were in a similar room. I am getting misty eyed. Kristina is a fine young woman.

I wonder if she is married. I have to find out. I am trying to take my mind off her because I am not in the mood to carry on an affair at this time in my life. I've been married three times maybe four. I think four is right, but that was way back. I am thinking of Kristina constantly now. She could be my associate, right? I don't have to marry her, and she might not even want to marry me, if she is single, right…? I'll just find out anyway, I tell myself. Maybe she has a football player for a husband, and he is going to kick the hell out of me if he finds out that I'm messing around with his wife.

Now I'm thinking about the incident at the Red Onion bar in Brantford. Good thing I had taken karate when I was in my thirties.

The Red Onion was the first time in my entire life that I actually had to use my WADO – KAI, martial art.

To stop worrying about imaginary jealous husbands and switch to something pleasant, I forced my mind to think about the launching pad they are building just outside of Brantford. I think the pad is to our advantage as it will attract a lot of extraterrestrial traffic. It'll be convenient for us to travel back and forth to Mars. I have thought of visiting some nearby planets like Mars. I can't think of any others that I should entertain. The trip to Mars is hard on the body. The speed is the killer and still it takes too long. I can take the eight hours to Mars and eight back but there isn't yet a heck of a lot to see or do on Mars. On the other hand in the future, it will be a different story. First things first. We have to make enough breathable air for the whole planet.

Just imagine hundreds or even thousands of gigantic ozonators made on earth and shipped to Mars. That's going to take a few months, maybe years. I'll leave that planet up to the scientists for the time being. It would be very nice too, if we could figure out how to travel by thought, like of the extraterrestrial aliens do. If we could do that, we could travel as fast as the speed of light, or faster. Then distance would mean nothing, and we could easily scout the whole universe. The reason we can't travel by thought is because we haven't invented the way to do that yet.

I can't stop thinking about Kristina, and I am surprised that she matters so much to me now. Maybe my DNA has something to do with that. One of my grandparents must have come from here many, many years ago. It would be interesting to know if my early relative was a man or a woman. I dreamily visualize Kristina in a yellow bikini dancing on the beach by a fire with her face painted white and her lips red. I am kissing her and holding her in my arms. She throws her head back and her red hair almost touches the flames. I loosen my grip on her as she slips from my hold and falls towards the fire but never falls in, just hovers over it. I reach for her with both my arms, as she circles the flames and then I grab hold of her. We are sitting on white sand, and we touch each other's face, arms bodies... I kiss and kiss her everywhere and we make love.

My phone is vibrating.

Kristina appears on the screen, smiling and saying, "You rang Charles? Are you at the Pegasus Hotel?"

"Yes, I'm in room number 307. You know where the hotel is?"

"Sure, I do Charles, I drive by it when I come to my school. I can be there in about twenty minutes; I have to finish off my day first."

I tell her we'll discuss the 'project' when she gets here.

I turn on the TV for noise and it is Joe Bonamassa and his band playing Boogie-woogie woman. I turn up the sound. I almost feel like dancing, but I turn to normal just in case she is 'flying' here. I can't believe how excited I am. I feel like a kid again. I can hardly wait for her.

Dreaming, reminiscing is like hesitating! But, but, I think I... I'm back on the stone and staring at the burning body in front of me. I want to wipe the rain from my face, but I can't move my hands! Luckily it isn't raining too hard. Obviously, this little rain has zero effect on the pyre. The pooling at my feet on the other hand bothers me. Rainwater from higher elevations could be collecting right here. I can't see the top of my shoes! They are under water. I can put my knees together and part them if I try very hard, but I can't move my feet too much up or down or sideways. I try to wiggle my toes, they are moving, but just a little. I'm scratching the side of my pants until my fingertips start to hurt. Maybe if I can scratch through my pants with my fingernails, my pants will fall off. Doing something is better than doing nothing. I am scratching my pants on both sides of my legs. This is going to take a long time. My fingers are hurting, and the nails are wearing down. The puddle is shimmering before me, and I can distinctly see all the rainbow colors of the oil on the top of the water. So, the rain comes and goes, it has stopped now. That's good. But I might burn to death if the oil catches on fire. The water is definitely rising around me. I can compare it to my shoes... it is now above my oxfords and my socks are soaked. There must be some stream feeding my puddle! The oil is in front of me, actually it is all around. Is it diesel or gasoline? Maybe I'll be alright if it is diesel or unprocessed crude oil. But it could be aviation fuel or gasoline...

A knock on the door switched the tracks for me. I jump up and tear the door open and the words 'hello Kristina' freeze in my throat. It is actually room service. I take the tray and I want to slip the person a crisp five-dollar bill but I realize it is a robot. I sit back on the bed instead.

The knock comes again, and it is Kristina. And she is hot... and so am I. We are two magnets connected instantly and stay connected for the next three hours.

CHAPTER SEVEN

"Charles, I am really happy that you found a school in Jamaica." Olly said as I entered his office. "Hope we'll be able to work with them". He said he had always had a difficult time getting things across to Klutch. "A lot of things he just didn't know. I am not a teacher I am a student," he said to me as he made himself comfortable on his grey leather chair in his guest room. He asked me to sit opposite him on the couch where we were having tea.

"You know Charles, when I said I probably knew you better than your mother did, I really meant it. When I located your cousin in Hungary, I found a gold mine. Can you figure out who I'm talking about?"

It took me a few seconds to think but suddenly it hit me.

"Mariska, you found my cousin Mariska, uncle Yany's daughter."

"But not just her, there were some others that still remembered you very well. Especially the person whose front tooth you knocked out in grade school. He is an old man now with a missing front tooth that he replaced with a gold one. To this day he still holds a grudge."

"You are kidding me Olly, that guy was a bully. I was just a skinny kid in those days, but I always had older friends who taught me well how to defend myself in a fight."

I guess Olly must have really been checking me out. Just the memory of that incident gave me a buzz on the top of my skull and the goosebumps travelled through my body right down to my legs and toes. That was the first time in my life I had to defend myself with my fists.

"Tell me what happened after you got off the boat."

"Things were a lot different when I arrived in Canada." I said, and I was going to tell him everything as it happened.

I didn't know what all he found out about the time I arrived in Canada as a lot of things have happened since. Actually, everything that has any significance happened after I arrived in Canada. Everything's in my head like it happened yesterday...

"So, then Olly," I started, "after an uneventful voyage on a ship called Ascania, we disembarked in Quebec City."

"What made you leave your country Charles?" Olly asked.

"I'll tell you, but this might take a little time." I cautioned him.

He said, "we've got all the time in the world."

"So, Olly, after I suffered through four months in a Yugoslavian holding camp, sleeping on straw-filled mattresses on three tiered metal beds, showering in cold water, drinking 'coffee' made from burned barley... and using the same enameled bowl for soup and greasy pork with potatoes. I always washed mine out with sand in cold water to get some of the grease off before the next morning's 'coffee'.

Anyway, one day a Canadian representative came, and I signed up to come to Canada. Another month or so later I was approved and along with other refugees, we sailed to Le Havre, then by train to Brantford Ontario."

"So, Charles why did you choose Brantford and not Toronto or some other larger cities? I had no idea about Canadian cities, their size or even location. I just thought Canada was a free country. I knew of an acquaintance of my parents living in Brantford and that is where I went.

When I arrived to the city, some government officials were waiting for me already at the train station and escorted me to a large building to an office where they put me through 'the ringer'. They told my acquaintance they'll call her when they get finished with me. They spoke English, I didn't understand a word.

For several hours these officials cross-examined me, 'interrogated' me at this place and held me incommunicado. I think that building was the Kirby hotel, that's what it was. I'll never forget that day. There were two or three men in uniform and one in civilian clothes. I can't remember their names but their expression and faces have remained engraved in my mind forever. I think the civilian's name was Bob, and he told me I wasn't under arrest just 'detained'. He spoke the Hungarian language.

They had somehow gotten my original dossier (kerdoiv) from my parents. I had no idea it even existed. They had it right in front of me – photo, signature, everything. In 1956 after the revolution, everyone's dossier was sent to their address and my parents must have gotten mine. I still have those documents today. Of course, I didn't yet speak English. They had a translator, Bob, sitting beside me who interpreted everything from English. I have to admit I looked pretty mundane in those days. I had a necklace on with a little gun that I fashioned out of Plexiglas myself. I remember to this day how meticulous a job it was to create. I worked on it for weeks to make it look perfect. Come to think of it, I really don't know what ever happened to that little gun. One day I just didn't have it anymore. I must have lost it. You can see it on a picture in one of the documents.

Anyway, the first thing they asked me was the same thing you asked me, 'Why did I leave your country?" I told them a little story.

Sounds weird now, but it was the truth. This is what happened on my very first day at a real factory where I was supposed to be working or learning 'observing' during the summer recess.

I went to school in Budapest. The local party commissar was one of my teachers who, for the longest time asked me to join the communist party. He was my Russian language teacher, and I excelled in that subject. Generally a person had to be endorsed by somebody, preferably by someone in a leading position. So, essentially, I was endorsed by the top man of the local *party*. Had I accepted the offer, maybe I wouldn't be here today. I could have become the Hungarian Prime Minister, or someone could have assassinated me by now. It is better this way, isn't it Olly? My dad wasn't in the party so I decided I wouldn't be either. I must have sensed there was something nefarious behind the scenes about communism that people didn't know about."

"Yeah, Charles, I read you." Olly said, fidgeting in his seat.

"I'll tell you the same story I told those officers. You're not going to believe it. In those days the fear of terror resonated everywhere. Rival political parties were abolished a one-party system was created. Individual ideas, views and expressions were banned unless they were to praise the glorious Communist Party. The weight of the iron curtain became a burden we could no longer bear.

My interrogators' eyes were popping, they had a hard time believing my story. When I started technical school, the country was under the worst kind of communist regime imaginable. Hungary's constitution was replaced with socialistic self-run government, patterned after the Soviet regime. They abolished private ownership, everything became centralized and ran out of money quickly. The shelves became permanently empty. Salt, sugar, bread, or milk could only be gotten with coupons. Everything became linked to politics and was run by politicians – by people who had no business knowledge, or any knowledge at all, let alone about commerce. Most of them were from the remote countryside, uneducated farm laborers doomed to failure right from the start. Some of them couldn't even write their name.

I was advised to observe experienced employees at work, learning how to do things the right way, Olly. The foreman at the plant told me to fraternize with 'outstanding' communist employees only.

How could I tell 'who is who' I asked? These employees have a red star pinned to their shop coats, or their caps. They keep their workbenches clean, uncluttered, treat other employees with respect, do their work diligently, arrive at the workplace early, spend their lunch breaks and eat their food in the main conference room, and more importantly listen to the uplifting messages of our courageous leaders and about our Great Communist Ideology.

I showed up in the conference hall a few times and when I didn't, I had a good reason why I wasn't there. I told my contact person that I was visiting other areas of the plant talking to other exceptional employees. His frown softened and turned into an approving, gentle smirk. I learned how to tell the slackers (none party members) from the heroic *good* employees apart. I approached employees that had at least one red star pinned to their shirt." With big eyes, Olly was staring at me.

"Now, listen to this, Olly. One day I was in this particular assembly area where they put machines together. As I am walking down an alleyway, I notice a 'three star' employee with a hammer in hand attaching certain parts to a machine. Assembly is usually done with a wrench or some power tool, I thought. He was assembling 'belt guards' and other attachments, everything that was supposed to be bolted onto the machine.

This assembler would start bolts in tapped holes and then he would drive them home with one good whack of his hammer. He had saved thirty minutes per machine by doing the job this way. On ten machines he saved five hours, a hundred machines in fifty hours and so on. No wonder he became a red star employee. That episode opened my eyes Olly."

He sat back in his seat and stretched his legs looking at me sideways. Then after a moment of hesitation he said, "I read you, Charles. I can see why you left your country. Communist leaders don't want too many smart people other than themselves. You must follow and abide by the _guidelines_. I guess you were going to talk about the Hungarian Revolution next, right?"

I was hoping he wouldn't ask me about that because I still have living relatives in the old country. I know everything is changed today, going in the right direction, but I would rather not make it tough for somebody else, and I told him that.

"You know how it is, Olly? You understand what I mean."

He said, "I do."

"To make a long story short, Olly, when the CSIS were done with me, they must have believed my story because they let me find a place to live in the city of Brantford, Ontario. They called my acquaintance who came to pick me up. They gave me spending money and gave me an opportunity to study at that prestigious place called the Westervelt College, where I received my 'Masters' diploma in Technology."

"I thought you had stayed at your parents' acquaintance's residence."

"No Olly, I went to live at a strawberry farmer's house in Cainsville. That place is roughly two kilometers from Brantford on highway #2. I befriended the farmer at the Blue Haven restaurant. His name was Ernie. He had cows and grew strawberries. I helped him on his farm in my spare time cultivating and picking berries. I wanted to make extra money to send to my parents back in the old country.

I was in the barn milking when lightning hit it and knocked me out cold. Ernie carried me into the house and called an ambulance. By the time the ambulance got there, I came to. The paramedic checked me over and told me I'd be fine. I survived without any problems. Then a month or two later the barn was hit the second time with me in it. But this time I didn't fall down I was just dazed and wound up with a headache. I can still hear the cows jumping back rattling the stanchions.

The third time the lightning struck me I was still at Ernie's place, outside in the yard, next to that infamous barn. I was working on my 1945 WWII Norton motorbike. I had rubber boots on, and I was holding onto a rubber handle grip. This time though I lost consciousness. Ernie had to pick me up off the ground where I had been prostate beside my bike."

"You know, Charles, I just want to say this, and I'm not trying to downplay the accidents but you're not the only one who got hit multiple times by lightning. There was a person who had been hit seven times. One time a bolt even burned a hole in his hat. That must have been something else."

"Yeah, Olly, I read that too in the 'Believe it or Not' book myself.

Do you want me to amaze you with the rest of my near-death experiences?"

George the robot server came and topped up our tea. "Sure, Charles, I'd love to hear them."

"Fasten your seatbelt, Olly. This goes back a few years. I couldn't have been more than seven when my class of twenty-five kids went to Lake Balaton. It was an all-day excursion, and we travelled by train. When we arrived, we were cautioned about the lake and let loose. We scattered like mercury from a broken thermometer.

Me and a little friend found a small rowboat and had decided to explore the lake on our own. It didn't take us very long before we got tangled up in a thick patch of reeds and cane where we tried to free the boat but upset it instead. The next thing I remember was somebody holding me by my feet, and I am puking water. The teacher thought I had drowned for sure."

"Well, Charles you were lucky. Your little friend must have hollered for help, and somebody came to save you. That wasn't the one whose tooth you knocked out, or was he?"

"No, no, Olly, the guy with the missing tooth came much later."

"I'm glad to hear that." Olly said.

"I was around ten or eleven when I was at this popular swimming pool and hotel in Budapest, the Gellert, where they had an artificial wave machine. I noticed every fifteen minutes it was activated. Being just a short little guy, I thought it would be a lot of fun to ride those waves. I went into the shallow end and suddenly more adults started to come in and somehow, they nudged me deeper and deeper into the pool. Soon I couldn't touch the bottom anymore. Not only that, but they all acted like flightless birds extending their arms, keeping themselves upright on top of the waves – pushing me even deeper until I stared to swallow water."

"Did you drown again?" "No, Olly. Somebody must have seen me struggling and rushed me out of danger."

"Well, you said you drowned twice, how did the second one happen?

"My second drowning disaster happened a year or two later."

"Let's hear it, Charles," Olly egged me on.

"I was at another swimming park splashing around having fun with my friends. We were in a shallow pool that was made for kids only. It had warm water in it and half of the water's volume must have been chlorine. You couldn't keep your eyes open when you went under. At the end of the day on my way out, like many times before, I stopped at a deep Olympic pool and at the edge of the pool I got down on my knees to lean into the water to get my hair wet to slick it back.

Someone came along and gave me a push and I went down like an axe without a handle. I remember taking one gulp of water, *one gulp* and blacked out instantly. Technically, Olly I was dead. Again, someone was holding me by my feet and I was puking water."

"This is ridiculous, Charles, why didn't you just swim out?"

"I didn't know how to swim yet, Olly."

He looked at me funny and shook his head.

I took a swig of my tea and started up again.

"The third time Olly, because I've drowned three times, I was about thirteen years old. I went by train to a neighbor's Mr. Pup's cousin's place – whom I played with when he came for a visit. About 150 km. from Budapest. The boy was my age.

We were at a stream splashing around, diving into the water off a pedestrian bridge. I still didn't know how to swim and of course it wouldn't have mattered, anyway. There was a large log in the water and some kid suggested that I should hang onto that for support. It made sense. However, the log was 'water logged'. When I was next to it, I could feel it without any problem. But when we were jumping into the water, I didn't see it and hit my head in it. Same old story again. Someone was holding me by my ankles and I was puking water."

"Charles, this is insane, you know you should have learned to swim after the first time you almost drowned?"

"I don't know why I didn't, Olly. This last time it wouldn't have made any difference, I simply didn't see the log. It was submerged in the water."

"So, when this was the third time you finally learned to swim."

"I did, Olly, but listen to this. A couple months before this happened, I had the most perilous episode of my life.

I was helping Mr. Pup in his 'belt buckle' shop on the other side of the street we lived on. One day he asked me to change a burned-out light bulb above his metal clad bench. I can just picture myself doing this. I took a stool to the bench, climbed up on it and grabbed the bulb with my right hand. With my left hand I got hold of the cable it was attached to. That bulb must have been there from the beginning of the century because it wouldn't budge. So, with my left hand I got hold of the socket which must have been conductive because I got electrocuted in that instant. I fell off the bench.

I was shocked by 220V DC. All I can tell you is that Mr. Pup bought me back to life because I'm here today. He never told me how he did it."

"This is truly remarkable, Charles.

Yeah, Olly I have probably passed out a dozen times thereafter. Every time they put me out in the hospital, I never knew whether I'd come back or not. Right?"

"Right, Charles."

"Anyhow, Olly, after I graduated from the Westervelt College I was immediately picked up by CSIS, (Canadian Security Intelligence Service) where I made good use of the different languages I'd learned. I took advanced Russian, Spanish and English, then later, when my *real* job started, I picked up one more, Arabic. I was actually fluent in Russian before I even came to Canada. I have met Stalin, and Khrushchev, Olly. I worked for CSIS as a 'secret agent' for a long time roughly thirty-five years – until I retired. My job with the *'Service'* included travelling to countries under different disguises, different names on different missions. I bet you didn't find out too much about me from this period, did you, Olly?"

Olly didn't answer that question just looked away smiling, but it wasn't a Yany smile, this was an understanding, approving sort of grimace and I knew he'd get my message. If he'd gotten any information about me during those years – that would have all been bad, bad for the people I worked with and for myself and everybody. He knew Canada always had to be 'the in between country', for good or for bad. Make peace in Yugoslavia, Kosovo, Middle East – Iran, Pakistan, Afghanistan, and China.

"Yeah Olly, I had to change names, my appearance my style. I really don't think anyone has ever recognized me with my 'then' pseudonyms."

"So then, Charles if you had retired how come you went back to working in that private company?

"I got bored Olly, when I *surfaced,* I got my old name back along with my old history. I got an offer from a private ISC, (International Security Company) and I worked for them for eight years then suddenly they went belly up – that's when you found me. Actually, the owner of the company had deceased, and the family bankrupted the company.

I had to stop for a moment or two to reminisce about those years with ISC… all the good times I had with that company. The golf tournaments, the comradery, the travel…

"That's the short and the long of it, Olly. Some of the work I did at ISC is the work you're interested in. Right?"

"Yeah, Charles but *all* the work you did interests me. I am interested in all of it, Charles."

"Ok Olly", I said, and I started from the time we left my grandparents and came back to Budapest. I carried on for an hour perhaps more without stopping.

I started with my father talking in hushed tones in our house even when nobody was around. Then after the war ended Hungary was run by Soviet style commanders the AVO, who shot, hanged, beat to death, or deported people. 'Subjects' who they didn't like went to forced labor gulags in Russia and another quarter of a million Jewish people were also sent to gulags in Russia. Justice became by government decree sparing no one, including political party leaders that were their former comrades, or their own siblings and parents. Other than the empty shelves, there was nothing in stores. Everything was restricted and on coupons. Tens of thousands of people were removed from Budapest and put to work on confiscated land. Their dignity stolen, their belongings, even houses expropriated family names changed to strange sounding pseudonyms.

I had to stop there, and Olly agreed because he could see the bad memories were starting to affect me in the wrong way.

I finished my cold cup of tea, stretched my legs, and got up from the couch and looked at Olly. He was shaking his head and said nothing.

I was in my office summarizing the Jamaican *project* when Olly came in and pulled up a chair close to my desk. In a happy tone he started, "Charles we are going to Medellin Columbia." He said that with a wide Yany as he sat down. "We are taking a regular flight."

I was shocked. I thought as usual we'd be flying in his private jet. He must have had a reason to fly public.

"Charles I'm going to tell you something that you should be very proud of. We've got the job. They bought our proposal, good work, Charles. I'm talking about 'the fish story'".

My jaw dropped from the moment he started talking and stayed dropped until he finished. I thought everything we did was top secret which went without saying. I thought he was going to tell me he was planning to bump somebody off, and I was happy that it only involved Columbia and Mexico. And they weren't starting a war but might as well have been.

"There is a multi-million-dollar tunnel being dug in Mexico, Charles, beneath the Rio Grande and the work is almost done. It was approved by the Mexican President and paid for by *a drug lord*. The drug lord is Cielito Wares or more affectionately called the Rat (Rata) in Spanish." Olly said.

I surmised it was a tunnel similar to the one between France and England. But I soon found out that wasn't the case. I thought it must be a tunnel from Mexico to the USA.

Then it dawned on me, this could be a tunnel to smuggle heroin underground. To me that tunnel business sounded like old hat, it had been tried before and had failed because it had been discovered. Surely, he's not going to try it again, and I mentioned this to him.

Olly smiled, coyly and went on, "the tunnel starts along the Rio Grande somewhere between Acuna and Nuevo Laredo and exits in the river in several different locations down towards the south."

Holy Moses, now it's getting a bit more interesting. To exit a tunnel in the river is different, in fact it is very novel, I thought.

Since the American President's new fence had partially been installed, Charles, it became more problematic to export drugs, to the USA the usual way. The dealers had to come up with a different way to ship their drugs. They are going to load fake carps and waterproofed bails with drugs and transfer them through the tunnel into the river. In Mexico there is a factory producing plastic carps already. When they arrive on the American side, programmed motors will take the schools of 'fake fish' down the river where they are caught by fishermen, always at different locations.

"The programming will be a song for you, don't you think, Charles?"

"Yes, yes," I answered bewildered and thinking how cool that was?

Olly paused for a little while, giving me time to let the story sink in. Then it hit me, I thought there was something wrong with that picture and I told him so.

"Who said there were carp in the Rio Grande, jumping carp no less?"

"There are no carp in that river yet, Charles but there will be.

There is an American company in New Orleans, 'R&M' that has been removing carp from rivers and lakes for decades. R&M

is acquired by the drug dealers. They'll 'milk' the eggs from the carp and broadcast them in the Rio Grande. They'll grow fast. They eat 50% of their body weight every week. The dealers' accomplices on the US side will fish in the river every day in different locations. They'll intercept the packages and reel the nets in with real carps along with the fake fish. Half of the carp will be dumped back into the river; the other half will go to the environmental company that makes them into fertilizer.

The drug dealers own that company too. This way they can ship even more drugs than before, and they will have a regular plant where they can 'process' the real fish and the fake plastic fish loaded with heroin." The fake fish are returned to Mexico.

My job was to come up with an indecipherable program that would signal the arrival of the 'schools of fake fish.'

The coded message of course, must only be received by dedicated personnel, the dealers that run the show.

I was never so taken aback in my life to hear a fish story like this. I had to hand it to Olly, he was indeed a genius man.

"In order to always have plenty of carp, they are bred and milked for eggs on the Mexican side. On the American side there will only be 'approved' contractors who will remove the invasive carp and make sure they'll never run out of them."

I tried to get my mind around the idea and poke holes in it. If there was a coordinated effort between the dealers and the 'fishermen' it could work. And I left it at that. Olly was quite excited about the project and told me so. I just sat there and listened. Sometimes I just nodded, other times I said something technical that he didn't understand but nodded approvingly, anyway. My head was full of ideas.

******

The pilot came on, telling us to buckle up because we are going to land at the El Dorado International Airport. I buckled up and wondered about the reception we were going to get upon our arrival. I wondered how many people knew about us coming. Probably a few, anyway. I was still amazed with Olly and the ideas he is getting from children.

CHAPTER EIGHT

As we disembarked the plane, a limo with dark windows was waiting for us. Olly asked me if I knew how many airports there were in Columbia. I guessed 20. He laughed and said there were 168 but the main airport was called El Dorado and that's where we were. They must have counted 'back yard' landing strips because there's no way a country can have that many legitimate airports, not for big jets, anyway.

The white limo came right to the plane to pick us up. The driver spoke perfect English, and he was a very amicable person. He was wearing a sidearm, partially concealed under his sports coat and he had an AR15 right between the two front seats. I knew we were going to be in a forest, but I don't think he had the gun to protect us from wild animals.

In about fifteen minutes we left the highway and drove into the jungle. He must have known where he was going. There was a wet bar on board, and we used it a couple of times. The blackened windows surely beat the alternative – a dark mask over our eyes.

The trip from the airport to the president's hacienda took about an hour. During this time the driver lowered the partitioned inside window and entertained us with stories of ancient ruins and some wildlife we've encountered.

When we arrived at this beautiful, sprawling paradise full of exotic birds and manicured shrubs, the enormous wrought-iron gate opened automatically.

As we drove up to the building, we passed a swimming pool occupied by playful young women, some whom might have been adorned by bikini bottoms. We could hear a mariachi band playing through the closed windows. As we got closer to the building, the band played even louder. The ladies in the pool were greeting us in Spanish, we assumed, and were jumping from joy, exposing themselves from head to toe.

The site could have even made Hugh Hefner blush if he were still alive. When we got out of the vehicle, there was an impeccably dressed female greeting us in bikini top and bottom and directing us into the house. She guided us into an elegant room where she offered us chairs to sit on. She told us the President would be with us in a few moments and asked us if she could fetch us some refreshments. Olly requested mango juice, and that was fine with me too. As I looked around in the room, I could see national culture and pride in several gold framed pictures and an iconic life-size portrait of El Presidente himself. Good taste combined with patriotic pride. In the adjoining room there were breathtaking eight-foot-high paintings of former presidents and of nature at its best. All paintings were framed in real gold.

In a short while two men entered, one was the drug dealer Rata, masquerading as the representative for the Columbian El Presidente. The other was the Mexican President Cordoba El Rio, who introduced himself. Both gentlemen spoke good English. We engaged in some pleasantries and elaborate introductions, after which we went into an adjoining room with the tall paintings where we all sat down around a granite table.

After a brief summary, Olly got down to business. On a white board at hand, he portrayed our elaborate plan and in a few sketches, he explained the crux of the system. The two gentlemen were enthralled. They even clapped after Olly's pleasant rendition. I didn't notice any video equipment but I'm sure there was some concealed behind the heavy curtains. In any case we didn't have to put on makeup like movie stars do.

"What I have here is highly confidential and top secret," Olly declared. "No one knows other than the two of us and now the two of you. My business is done on a one-on-one basis. We are the engineers, and we supply the solution to your problem. We design the operation and guarantee that it will work. For how long? Who knows until it's discovered?

The gentleman you see here is an extension of myself, talking to him is like talking to me. So, feel free to engage him in the future, when I'm not available or incapacitated in any way."

I stood up and took a bow. The two presidents nodded in unison and said to Olly, 'the cheque will be in the mail'. Olly had no doubt about that.

Once the meeting ended, we were invited to a swimming pool party where the mariachi band played again, even louder as they saw us coming out of the building. We declined but sat under a large umbrella and enjoyed the flowers and the birds and the occasional visit from a few of our charming hostesses in their uniforms of nothing until we were called in for dinner. The music was great, and the food was excellent but so, so hot that even I could hardly eat it. Olly cleared his throat and rubbed his eyes a few times and left most of it on his plate. He ate the desert.

We could have stayed overnight if we had wanted to, could have watched the acrobats twirling down flagpoles, watched the magicians and listened some more to the upbeat Mexican music, but Olly was anxious to go, and I didn't argue with him. We were seated in the same limo as we came in, a Cadillac. We also had the same chauffeur. I enjoyed the ride and thought about the conversation we had with the driver on the way in. I remembered asking him what university he went to in the USA, he said Yale.

While Olly was deep in thought, my mind was already working on the coded system and even if he asked me, there wasn't much I could tell him now, because most of the stuff I was involved with was highly technical. What would he know about ANI, AGI, ASI, or the massive machine language I would have to create for our *project?*

The partition was up in the car, but Olly put two fingers on his lips, and I got the message. We spoke in a guarded voice we didn't discuss anything related to business, especially strategies and how to protect my software from hackers, default limitation, and more importantly, how much, if any, of the software our clients would be interested in having. We decided not to give our client any information about the software, it would complicate proceedings. If the system works for any length of time, we are in the clear.

Our plan is based on an idea, an assumed idea, nonetheless.

Easing the partition down, our driver told us that planes to the USA were flying every hour so we could wait in the car, or he could let us in the departure area. We took the latter.

Something jerked me back to my stone seat and my hopeless situation. Olly wanted to talk about an important matter. I pretended to listen, but my mind forced me to get back to the burning body in front of me.

The rain is pouring again, and my fear tells me to pay attention to my predicament. It is coming down so hard now that I have to keep my eyes closed. "What's going to happen to me" I cry out in complete desperation. My voice sounds feeble in this pitiful realm. Is it possible for a sane person to suddenly go crazy? I don't know. But it could happen. I could imagine that I'm well and normal. But that would be hard to take. It is easier to think that someone abducted me. I must be in some country that I have been in before and someone recognized me. Have I been abducted by robots? Impossible! Robots are machines and machines can't abduct people because they are not programmed to do that, and robots can't think.

The water is coming pretty close to the top of my stone seat and smells like diesel. Diesel does not catch on fire easily and it doesn't have to. If it reaches my chin or my mouth, I have to swallow, swallow diesel? Maybe I can breathe through my nose for a while then I'll be finished, I'll be a goner. I can agitate the water by moving my feet up and down, but the turbulence means nothing… moving my feet faster is very tiring. The rain's slowing down now, and I hear the humming sound of a drone. I hope it's an Autonomous Flying Robot AFR. Hopefully it comes from Olly because he is searching for me! But if it isn't Olly, who else would be concerned about me then? Klutch? Are the perpetrators checking on me? It could be an adversary, could be an enemy who wants to see if I'm still alive. See if I'm still moving. Should I try to move, or scream, or shout? There's absolutely nothing I can do. In fact, it is better if I don't do anything. I can't make myself look any smaller or larger. I can yell, or should I? A drone has cameras and can observe a large area, depending on how high it flies. If it is friendly, it will see me and the burning body, probably the body first. If I'm not on fire, it might not even notice me. I can't wave my arms; I can splash the water and create some disturbance.

On the other hand, what if it is my tormentors. In that case I'd better sit still. Pretend to be dead. That is my best bet. If I could see it, I could tell if it was armed, but I can't see a drone or anything. Maybe it is on the opposite side of the burning corpse hidden by smoke. Can't even see the drone past the smoke. It has to come around!

It must come around if Olly sent it. If it is the enemy's flying robot, they only need one with a weapon, I'm going nuts.

The rain has stopped, but the water is still rising! I'm in a valley, no question about it. The corpse is definitely on higher ground. I still can't see the drone. It doesn't make much sound at all, maybe it isn't even a drone, just my imagination. If there was a pipeline explosion, there will be workers coming around to shut the valve off. But then if there was an explosion the valves should have shut off automatically. Any drop in pressure should shut the valves off. I must think positive. An explosion must have happened very recently, or it happened close to the valve. That might take days before they come around to fix it. Will I last for days? Will I drown in hours?

I can't close my eyes when I listen to noises, it is the same sound all the time. To me even the smallest change from the hissing sound would make a difference. I noticed the flying robot. But that's it, just one AV.

I've got to figure out where I am. I keep telling myself to think, and that is exactly what I'm doing. I just can't think any harder.

I'll check to see if my computer knowledge will help.

But it's all zeroes and ones…all around me, and water. Here comes a bunch of ones. Now zeroes…

CHAPTER NINE

On our way home without any delay the plane taxied out and quickly gained altitude. I looked out the window and watched the verdant green getting smaller and smaller behind us. The monotonous humming sound of the jet engine usually puts me to sleep. But I was awake when Olly started talking about the life cycle of a tiny poppy seed. The loud music of the mariachi band was still playing in my ears, and I became confused. My mind became scrambled. My mind tells me to listen to Olly, but I harken back to the burning body that is hissing, humming? Where am I?

I'm sitting here attached to this stone and forcing myself to remember something to take my mind off my miserable situation.

I am right back in the clinic after the fight at the Red Onion. I am waiting for the doctor to bandage me up. I'm thinking of my prospective employer and the meeting I have with him. I hope I'll be all healed by then. I am looking at the cover of a Reader's Digest magazine. The headline is talking about the *benefits of self-care* on the cover. ...I was sitting in the waiting room ... I must have been. I am almost in exactly the same situation now, except my face was hurting then, now I'm hurting all over. My whole-body aches as if I had been given a bad drug or been run over by a truck.

If I remember correctly, the Reader's Digest advised 'How to handle anxiety with yoga.' I never expected to use even the thought of yoga. I should have paid a lot more attention to that story. Olly is calling out my name repeatedly. I can see him leaning back in his seat legs crossed. Am I going crazy already, now...?

Through the engine noise, or drone noise, I hear Olly begin, "Charles I'm sure you must have handled a few drug cases in your day, but I'd put this poppy issue right up at the top." Ok, he's talking about heroin.

"After I googled the information on the poppy seed, I was truly amazed. I was astounded with all the monikers they gave this innocent poppy seed – it really blew my mind, Charles.

And just to disregard the seed all together, think about our clients who are more interested in the pods than the seeds especially when they are still green, and the seeds are just starting to form. Did you know, Charles that one little seed alone is enough to grow one pod and produce enough heroin to cause death to several addicts? I am talking about heroin as we all know it. Charles, are you ok?"

I am thinking 'Reader's Digest' meditate…

But I have to answer Olly. Did he ask me something? I am not sure if he asked a question or not. I think he was talking about a poppy seed or heroin. I took a chance and answered as if I knew what he was saying.

"Yeah, Olly I came across a few addicts in my time too, but they usually involved the underworld dealers and occasionally the victims. I wasn't too interested in how the product was produced. I remember my mom using ground poppy seed and making cakes with it. But of course, mom and I were talking about poppy seed as food. I remember saying this."

"Yes Charles, the use of the poppy seed in the confectionary business is entirely different. A lot of people would go hungry if the poppy seed was used for food only. Take most of the Mid Eastern countries where the illegal poppy is grown, and the population is poor and easily persuaded to producing the right kind of poppy for heroin. Many times, as you know, it takes more than kind words to make illegal things happen. Most of the time the tar or milk or 'latex' whatever name the substance is called in that region is processed by kids, young children. Imagine, the poppy flower is pollinated by bats, not bees. These bat colonies live in caves in Texas and Mexico and Columbia. These bats number in the tens of millions and they come out to catch billions of insects every night. Charles, the illegal operation is under the jurisdiction of designated governors, cartels and followed to strict order. Not abiding by the unwritten laws can be brutal, often deadly."

"Yeah Olly, everything has to be approved at the top. On the other hand you can be an elected symbolic president too, but that doesn't mean you call all the shots. No sir. You are the president on paper only. You can be called president, prime minister, king, sultan, or cardinal."

"Yes, cardinals aren't angels either." Olly said.

"That's right Olly. I too did some business once with a cardinal myself."

"I can't get over this magical plant, Charles. Apparently, there is a great difference between geographic regions, soils and climates where this poppy is grown. In certain locations exact amounts of fertilizer must be used. Some plants ripen faster than others, even in the same field. The height of the plant may vary from 30cm to 150cm. The color of the flowers can also be different starting from light pink to dark blue."

"Where do you think they get the seeds, Olly?"

"That is a good question, Charles. There's got to be a way they can tell what seeds to use. I'm sure of that."

Olly stopped and thought for a little while.

"Some people can tell Charles. The cartels have all the power to select the right farmer who knows the difference from seed to seed.

The latex must be collected just at the right time too, keeping in mind the weather conditions. Too much rain can wash the latex off, and heavy winds can flatten the crop. Early frost can kill the whole crop overnight. It is not the easiest plant to grow.

Our job concerns the delivery of the base product, only the delivery of heroin. You might ask me why just heroin? Why not cocaine and heroin? I'll tell you why Charles. Heroin is the lesser of the two evils.

Heroin has antidotes cocaine hasn't.

They're both cheap to produce and become valuable only after they arrive in America. In America heroin has many names, it could be called smack, thunder, brown sugar, junk, hell dust, just to name a few. Everything depends on how the base is broken down.

Cocaine is entirely another story, Charles. You overdose with crack cocaine you are dead for sure.

Furthermore, we are interested in the *transportation* of heroin only. Trump's wall really threw the monkey-wrench into the gears.

I had to figure out a secure way to get the product into the USA.

Cocaine takes a different route, it comes from the south, usually via the Gulf of Mexico. Had it involved cocaine I wouldn't have touched it.

The fake fish was my idea, Charles. I invented the method of transportation myself. Up until now, Charles, I did all the thinking, however from now on I want you to get your feet wet and handle some of the situations on your own."

"So, the carp was your idea?"

"Yes, it was. They just wanted to pack heroin into fake fish. That might have been alright too, but the carp is definitely a better choice."

"How did you come up with that brilliant idea, Olly?"

"Charles, you looked at me funny when I mentioned Klutch, the kids in schools, playing and creating often overrated games with mostly outdated toys or computer games, and I understood your surprise. You probably thought I was a little crazy.

When kids look at toys or other things in a store, their minds are working. They think of what they can use the toy or the item they are looking at for. They are converting the toys into games or into something they can build.

We adults think differently, we use logic right, Charles. We don't just look at things, we observe them. We understand what gadgets do and what they are used for.

Let me tell you how this fish story evolved. When you came back from Jamaica, you said 'the kids were watching a segment about jumping carp do you remember?"

"Yea, Olly I remember."

"There were hundreds of fish jumping into boats, into empty baskets. I think the teacher asked the kids 'how many different ways can you catch fish'? Right, Charles?"

"That's right, Olly."

"One kid said, 'with a beer cooler.' Everyone howled with laughter. You remember, Charles?" I smiled and nodded.

"I liked you because 'you too have to always win' and I liked your moniker, the three D-s."

"But Olly, surely you don't really think that El Rata will get away with the carps for very long?"

"It doesn't matter, Charles."

"As you see, I didn't put any time limitation on the project."

"I noticed that, Olly. That was a smart move. They loved the idea. It will probably take a few years before the US government finds out what's really going on out there."

"You have to always take risks, Charles. I don't like drugs either. But this way we give a lot of people, I mean a hell-of-a-lot of people work, put bread on their table and we control the outcome.

Right, Charles?"

"Right, Olly."

I didn't know it at the time, but when he was finished talking, I understood a lot more about Olly. He looked out the window absent mindedly.

I looked out the window too, but I thought about meditation. Meditation, how do I *meditate*? Clear your mind of everything!

Don't think about what Olly said or what anybody said. Now I hear people shouting at me, egging me on to clear my mind, clear your mind!... I'm back on the stone again.

CHAPTER TEN

Cocaine heroin, addiction… memoir my beautiful daughter, my son… my heart is breaking.

The next two page(s) of this chapter have been left open for those who have lost loved ones to any of these illegal *drugs*. This is your book, your words, your thoughts will memorialize your story, a sad one, no less. Writing down your feelings and experiences can be quite challenging. There are hundreds of definitions attached to these illegal drugs, monsters and their names are on your computer or on your personal device, in many different languages. Out of my compassion I will not give them any more acknowledgement.

You can simply start:

THIS IS MY STORY (your desired name). You can write down your comments or write a book, you decide.

CHAPTER ELEVEN

Why am I chained to this stone. Do they want to starve me to death or drown me? Why me and not Olly? This is Olly's business. I am only working for him. He can answer a lot more questions than I can. He knows everything. He has been in this business all his life. He said his family had been manufacturing armaments since the first WW.

He knows everything about wars and everything that is going on. I just started to work for him. He didn't tell me what all he did in his life. Or is it me *they* are after? Someone from my previous occupation recognized me and wanted to get revenge for something I did to them. Am I paying for my old sins? That is possible! The longer you live, the longer your sins live too?

Most people get old and die. Your terrible mistakes, your evils, wanton desires, your unspeakable deeds vanish and die with you. Nobody is going to punish an old general for sending thousands to their death for no gain to themselves. Nobody's going to blame a lover for abandoned romances. But if you're aged and you don't look old, they not only remember your face, but they remember your sins too. So, if you don't look old when you get old, get a face job to make you look older by a lot. Then no one's going to recognize you, and nobody will even talk about you because they think you passed on a long time ago. Otherwise, they'll get you. You have to fess up, because you can't hide your mind! Your mind remembers where and when whatever you did, and you confess, give away everything, your mind pleads guilty. And *the* machine will prove it. Then you're done – *kaput*.

Technology is so far advanced today that reading someone's mind is a walk in the park. Special equipment is required, but it is a machine, and the machine can do all the work. If you have the money, you can get that machine. You are incapable of hiding anything that is in your mind. Even if you meditate, you're not able to disguise your sins!

If you are writing something on a computer that you don't want to keep when you're done, make a copy then delete it, get rid of it. Even at that rate all computers retain what you wrote. Anything you do is recorded somewhere. I start thinking again.

Slowly I'm trying to move my right foot out of my shoe, and something is working. Now I'm happy that my shoes *are* in water. Maybe I can free my foot. The water made my shoes softer, more flexible. I am taking my time. Don't have to rush anything. Sliding my right foot back and forth in the oily water, back and forth... I think I can do it. Now I'm glad there's oil in the water, maybe I can slide my foot out of the shoe and maybe my foot through the clamp. Easy... easy, moving my foot sideways, very tiring. Let's try my left foot. Get the shoe off, the sock is a problem. Maybe on the right foot... the sock, if I could remove the sock... I'm pressing my heel against the stone and the sock is bunching up, not coming off! I push the shoe away and now my sock is rolling back up. If I flatten my foot, maybe I can get it through the two-part shackle. Luckily the two-part shackle ring is made to fit all sizes. My ankles are skinny, my foot is narrow, and should slide through the ring.

The oily water is getting higher, it is just under my knees. I'm sitting in water now. The clamps on my hands are at the same level as my behind.

Actually, I am surrounded by oily water and hoping the oil won't catch on fire and start to burn. I can feel the oil between my fingers. Yes, if my fingers are slippery from the oil, my toes would be too. I hope I won't lose the ability to carry on, I must carry on, have to survive. I am scared. I'm terrified. I imagine the fire getting closer. I can already feel the heat. I smell the burning body – my own. I imagine my own burning body smells like charcoal or oil. I can smell the burning flesh even through the rain. I am imagining all this and know that I'm close to losing my mind. I have to stop working myself up into a frenzy. There is no fire, at least not yet. I am raising my knee higher and twisting my foot a little to the left, to the right. Keep repeating it, but I have to rest. One more time… my right foot is out, my foooooottt iiisss oouuuuttt from the clamp. I can't stop jubilating. Voila!

I can now assist my left foot out of the shackle. I have to push my right shoe away. My bunched-up sock, is off too. I take one hell of a breath. I am not religious but say it anyway - thank you God. No problem, the left foot is out too. Voila, voila. I could jump for joy.

Now let's see what I can free next.

I can't keep my eyes off the burning body. My T-shirt. Where did my T-shirt come from? A green T-shirt with a personal carrier pictured on it… The water is accumulating pretty fast, it's almost up to my belt. Both of my feet are free. Somehow, I've got to get my hands free too. I have to devise a plan. Slow down! Relax.

I'm trying to think, but Olly creeps into my mind instead. Why am I thinking about Olly? He has finished with the poppy seed story, and we are still on the airplane – he clears his throat and looks at me shaking his head as if he was fighting with himself about what he had done. He did something bad, created a monster. But then he swallows his bile and asks me if I ever smoked marijuana. I'm not going to lie, so I tell him the truth. I told him I tried it out of curiosity about forty years ago and I mentioned Adrian again, and he remembered. It was illegal then. The couple of drags I took from somebody's cigarette didn't have any effect on me, so I forgot about it.

He gives me a wide Yany. He said in Canada, marijuana is fast becoming an internationally approved commodity. It is so widely used that everyone, even children can enjoy the product and benefit from it. He was thinking of CBD products I figured, not the dope that people smoked. Senor Rata was shipping opioids and not marijuana. Today, in Canada anybody can grow all the cannabis they want. I am thinking.

I'm very excited about the progress that I've made after removing my shoes.

I don't know if Olly could tell, but I'm not paying any attention to him. And of course, I'm not, because that happened at a different time. We were flying over Cuba as Olly started talking about all the extraterrestrial traffic we've encountered lately. They don't come here for drugs, I'm sure. And now, I can't believe this, I'm remembering something... that must have really happened.

Olly and I are coming back from Columbia. We are landing at the Jose Marti airport to pick up passengers.

The plane taxied close to the terminal buildings and had stopped for too long, twenty or thirty minutes. Suddenly, three plain clothed G2 policemen saying something to the pilot and stepped into our cabin but the pilot didn't speak Spanish. Luckily a stewardess that came in with them did. She said we had to get off the plane because there's a problem. Olly and I stated that this was an illegal act, and we didn't want to comply. The Cuban officials said the plane was impounded and wouldn't be allowed to leave until we got off.

Olly couldn't believe what was happening.

A million thoughts flooded my mind including this brazen kidnapping by Cuban authorities. Olly suggested that we'd get off the plane if he was allowed to call his lawyer on his smartphone.

As we stepped off the airliner the police asked for our passports which we handed over immediately.

"Gentlemen you… are detained … temporally, of course, but you have to follow us please. The gentleman (and he pointed at Olly) can make a call once we are off the plane."

I was told to follow the police into the terminal, Olly was led into a room that appeared to be empty. I looked over his shoulders and saw no one inside the room. That was the last time I saw Olly.

I was nudged down the hall into another room which too was empty. The policemen didn't come in, but I heard the door lock click behind me. I was stressing my brains out trying to remember if I had done something nefarious to someone in Cuba. I didn't think I'd been to Cuba before.

Immediately I remembered Che Guevara, a Marxist Argentinian revolutionary who was killed by the Bolivian army. But that was a long time ago, and I was sure they were not going to blame his demise on me. I had all kinds of horrific episodes racing through my mind, most of them happened in the Middle East. I saw executions by drones, by hangings, waterboarding and downing but none of them fit this scenario.

In about ten minutes the door opened and two men in civilian suits came in, both wearing facemasks. They handed one to me too and told me to put it on. Then they started talking and decided to have the masks off and allowed me to take mine off too.

The room was about twelve by twenty feet with a painted brown desk that was close to the far end of the room with three chairs on the outside and one chair between the wall and the desk. It was an ideal room for interrogations. There was one picture in the middle of the room and that was of Che Guevara, the first person that came to my mind when I thought about the reason I was here.

They asked me to sit down on the single chair, while they took two of the three on the opposite side of the desk.

One of the two official put his forefinger to his lip signaling me to hold my mouth shut. The other spoke roughly to me in English and told me that they were going to do the talking and I was going to do the listening.

I immediately objected and asked for our lawyer.

They said they would let me have a lawyer in due time.

They asked me my name, the company I worked for and other things that I didn't want to tell them or didn't know the answer to.

This took about fifteen minutes. One looked at the other and the one that was looking asked me if I was vaccinated against COVID-19, and I told him that I was. In any case they had a doctor who was going to give me a needle just to be on the safe side.

I objected, but they dismissed me and one of them went to the other corner and made a call on his phone.

The other guy who stayed with me showed his palm and stated regulations. I called him an asshole under my breath.

In about three minutes a white coated individual came in with a tray and a needle and a vile that was supposedly be the COVID-19 vaccine or rat poison. I know I stood up to take off my jacket to hang it on the back of the chair. They told me to sit down and roll up my shirtsleeve. I did that on my left arm and that was the last thing I remembered.

They escorted Olly back to the plane and told him to shut up as this has nothing to do with him. It was me they wanted. Olly was beside himself.

He flew back home and started to pull strings immediately.

He had heard of the mysterious buzzing sounds in Cuba and wondered if I was subjected to them myself.

In the meantime, I had been taken to several different locations and injected with 'truth serum' and was questioned systematically.

I was accused of the killing of General Quassim Suleimani and his aid Abu Mahdi al Muhandis at a Baghdad airport. I had nothing to do with that missile strike. I was drugged or injected several times during the next three or four days. I was force fed at least once a day and had peed myself several times.

I have no idea what I agreed to or what I denied. My mind must have been mush.

At my old company I was no angel. To them I must have been like the others on the stones they had lined up in a row behind me. One thing for sure, when they were finished questioning me, I don't know if I was placed on the stone below a hill on purpose or if I was just lucky that that happened to be the spot I got when the dice were rolled.

I'm sure as hell lucky it worked out this way.

I could have been one of the people behind me and they are all dead. They have drowned on oil laden rainwater.

Now that my legs are free from the shackles I can start thinking of my hands. But now I have to figure out how to get the clamps off my hands. If I could bend my right leg up and reach over to my left side and push out the pin that holds the clamp on my hand that would do it. I'm trying my damnedest.

I'm not nimble enough anymore but I'm sure I'll be able to do it if I try hard.

I keep on trying. I'm getting tired. Have to rest. I can twist my body now and this helps my foot get closer to the rectangular tapered pin in my hand cuff. It's working! A little bit at a time... it is going to work.

Where am I now? My brain screams.

"The aliens are machines," Olly says, "just like the UFOs, pre-programmed machines. The extraterrestrials can't show emotions. Not only that, but they are totally impervious to any medical conditions, diseases like cancer or COVID-19, influenza, or any other debilitating human illnesses."

This happened before the plane landed in Cuba. How come I'm thinking in reverse?

"But they can be carriers Olly." I'm saying. My thoughts are jumbled.

Olly's looking out the window while I force myself to think how in hell, I am going to undo my belt. Maybe I don't have to worry about my belt. It must be fastened to the bar behind my back. That's why I can't lean forward. There's a chain that goes through a ring in the rear. And the hand cuffs are welded to the chain.

I have to start on my hands first. Am I flexible enough to reach the cuff on my hand with my foot? Yes. These clamps are the same as the ones that were on my ankles except the cuffs are smaller and they have a pin in them to keep them closed. Hook and staple situation. These have pins in the staples. If I twist my body, I could reach the head of the pin. If I could just bend my knee a little more. I'm trying to reach the head of the pin with my toe. Won't work this way. See if I can get one of my shoes up here and use it for a tool. I'm happy about the oil in the water. I'm feeling around with my feet for my shoes and find one of them. Now to get it up here… come on! Come on! Hook my right toe into the shoe, lift it into my lap. Push it over my leg, bend the leg over towards my left hand. I'm so glad I kept up with my exercising. I seem to be nimble enough to bend every which way. I can put the shoe down and rest. I listen to more of Olly's story.

"Our aliens must have learned signaling from us. On approval, nodding their head vertically, disagreeing by moving their head sideways. Did you notice that too Charles?"

"Yeah Olly, I too noticed that. Not much chance for getting help to cure anything from the extraterrestrials. They are machines. We are barking up the wrong tree Olly. But I tell you just keep your eyes on our cannabis. Its magic is unlimited."

I grab a hold of a shoe again with my toe and push it up around my lap, line it up with the pin. Now to push out the pin. It is going to work but I have to rest. If I was thirty years younger, it would be a synch.

"I think cannabis will cure cancer someday."

Olly says that half believing, sort of. I believe it 100%. In fact, I advocate it.

Olly clears his throat and goes on, "yeah Charles, in Canada an entirely new taxation system had been created and approved by successive governments. This new money is tremendous for roads and long neglected infrastructure. Health care, education and interplanetary sciences will greatly benefit from it too. Everything will be financed with this newfound wealth. Canada, with millions of acres of land will became the new 'Promised Land'. From new foreign investments to tax shelters, it will be hard to beat. Any prime minister will know that."

The pin's moving a little, maybe the next attempt. Olly continues.

"Even the property taxes will be greatly reduced and, in some places, completely eliminated. Isn't that something? Isn't that great? Have you heard about the new landing strip planned for the Brantford Airport? Construction is well on its way now Charles."

"No, Olly, that's going to be the launch pad for 'Interplanetary Vehicles Park and Descend' (IVPAD)."

"Oh, I guess you're right. Charles. Apparently when you go to Mars, the duration of travel has been reduced to eight hours thanks to Lincoln Alexander Hoffmann.* Have you ever heard about this guy?"

"Yes. Olly." I said and went on "I read his biography. He was inventing things in grade school already. I understand he was also awarded the Nobel Prize for the H&TI (Hurricane & Tornado Interceptor). He is better than Elon Musk I hear."

"Hoffmann is building robots that travel to planet E28 Charles. He is building robots similar to our visiting UFOs. Aerial travel is getting faster and being reduced by several light years at a time. I understand he is working on something even more remarkable than Einstein's theory."

"He's the man that can do it, Olly."

I'm trying to position my shoe heel against the pin.

"Yeah, Charles. Einstein is stuck with e=mc2 and this works on earth, but spaceship travelling with the speed of light is the thing. Whatever time it takes to get to your destination it will take the same coming back. I'm trying to push the pin with the heel of the shoe, but I *can't* push very hard with the waterlogged shoe.

The buzzing sound of a drone drowns out the hissing noise of the burning body. What in hell is going on out here?

Now I hear a faint sound, someone is saying something… we…will…come. We know where you are… I can feel the buzz in my arm. …We are coming to ge…t y..ou. We are reading your chip.

I can't believe it. They have found me. They gave me the signal; I can feel the slight vibration on my arm. They have recognized me. The same feeling, I had when I met Olly and he put his hand on my shoulder. Now an even stranger feeling overwhelms me. It feels like there's a screen in my head, and someone is turning it on and off. Someone is operating this screen by hand and closing in on specific items. Yes, it is either a computer monitors or a TV screen. Somebody is using a strong light sweeping over a large terrain, a disaster area. The searchlight illuminates a wide area.

I can see a drone taking a video of me and another drone with three tiny blue dots hovering. Now the camera switches to the drone above me. I can see the burning corpse too, which is not really burning, rather it is the busted gas pipe burning about thirty feet away from the body. There is oil or gas gushing out of the pipe that has not been blown up but had come apart. So, on the top of the rain this low-lying area is filling up not just with rainwater but oil as well. Boy am I happy or what, I got the shackles off.

I can see two drones with identical three blue lights… one is texting to me.

Now a loudspeaker - WE WILL GIVE YOU A SIGN WHEN WE COME TO GET YOU. I can read this in the cloud screen before me. …WE…ARE ENCOUNTERING INTERFERANCE WITH OTHER DRONES AND A FLOCK OF UNMANNED AERIAL ROBOTS. OUR ROBOTS HAVE THREE SMALL BLUE LIGHTS. Remain on your seat! Don't move. Blink your eyes three times now if you can hear me. Ok, blink three times if you can notice three blue dots on me now. Great we can communicate. I blinked three times, but I must carry on. I must get the hell out of everything.

Now I need to know when they are coming to get me. I can still drown. Maybe I'm ok, the pin is pushed out of the shackle. I can remove the right shackle with my left hand. Now they are both off. All I have to take off is the belt. The shackle chain is looped through a two-inch diameter ring on the flat bar which is against my back. The bar has the ring welded to it in the rear and my shackle's chain feeds through it. The belt around my stomach has holes in it, the other part has a buckle with a pin, just like in a regular belt. I have a belt like that in my closet it's made of hard canvas.

So, this is adjustable, just like a real belt. They think of everything. No problem. The belt is off. But I must stay seated and keep the ring over my head. Actually, it was just an ordinary ring to keep my head straight. It has a single rounded bar to keep my head from moving up. I see flashes in the burning body's direction and the body is really not burning, the leaking gas or oil pipe is – about thirty feet away from it. Ok, I'm not going to drown or burn now, but how am I going to get away from here, where am I? I sit back down. Am I back on the plane now?

"If we could travel by thoughts... figure it out yourself Charles." Olly is saying. "Suppose you want to go to Toronto, think it, and you are there. Suppose you want to go to the moon, think it, and you are there.

You can even go to the moon, to the place Neil Armstrong and Buzz Aldrin landed, and you are there.

Say you want to go to Mars, bingo you are there. Or planet Europa, you are there. Or planet E28, bingo you are there. Isn't that a heck of a lot faster than Einstein's speed?"

I want to agree but I don't know who I'm talking to. I need directions out of here.

Is this Olly talking to me again, I am asking myself?

He is asking me "did you hear about the close call with the John F. Kennedy carrier and some amphibious USO-s (Underwater Submersible Objects) diving in the Pacific Ocean where the carrier was maneuvering? I'm damn sure they communicate with us but that's top secret. They are a hell of a lot more advanced than we think they are."

"I think the aliens were just showing off, Olly, they were STUNT DIVING."

Why am I thinking about the conversation with Olly? But I have to wait to see what is going to happen next.

There are more flashes up above, as if there was an aerial war between drones and UAV's almost like in my 'recurring dream'. Maybe this IS my recurring dream now. Everything has changed to modern times. The tracer bullets are crisscrossing, this time it is the dying aerial drones that are spinning out of control. The smoke is coming from flying machines in the sky. Look out! Look out, LOOK OUT CHARLES screams a mechanical sound. The drones are going down, spinning, caterwauling, regaining power for a second or two, then flying off to the side mortally damaged. Some drones try to make it on one or two propellers. They are only wallowing in blackened mud flashes in real time, on my screen. There are thousands of broken down roachbuts and batbuts and defenderbuts all over the place. As I move my head, the screen moves too. I'm looking forward, towards the body... there is nothing behind my 'burning' corpse companion but jagged stumps. An enemy quadcopter aerial robot is spewing out gum like streams and the gum is getting onto propellers, slowing them down. Here comes one now, zoooms away and splashes into the water right beside me. The propellers turn once, then twice more, splashing, and trying to get out of oily water. I can't see if it is ours or the enemy. It makes no difference I have to sit back on my stone and wait for directions.

CHAPTER TWELVE

It is pouring now, I can't even keep my eyes open it's raining so hard. What's going to happen next? The water is well above the stone seat, if I hadn't freed myself, I'd be worrying myself to death. I would definitely be sitting in water. I can't think of a reason why I should be here. Olly has something to do with this situation, he must have. He keeps coming back into my head.

If I think hard enough, maybe I can push the reset button in my mind and default back to him or to Kristina the same way as he showed me on the holograms at the office. The only problem is that I'm not in the office.

At least now I know how to take my mind off this predicament that I'm in. When I fumble all, I have to do is think of something pleasant. But then I used to feel down all the time sitting on this blackened stone. I can now watch the action above me and in front of me. Am I being defended by unmanned aerial vehicles? What is going on out here? Looks like this territory is being invaded or defended.

Someone seems to be winning, I hope it is our side. An aerial battle is going on in front of me, just to the left of the burning body. Three blue dots. That's us.

I hear some voices from above, and in real time … someone is directing me, my heart drops – I see three blue lights "REMAIN AT YOUR LOCATION, WE ARE UCAV (unmanned combat aerial vehicles) - DO NOT MOVE".

"SENDING for IRD, GO AHEAD, IRD. (International Rescue Drone.)

"IRD, ARE YOU MOBILE, CHARLES? IF YES – MOVE AN ARM".

I'm hearing conflicting commands. "CONFLICT! Disregard UCAV command, MOVE AN ARM. Ok. "We've copied your location. DON'T MOVE ANY MORE".

I hear all kinds of noises; buzzing, exploding, winning, multiple gunshots, almost like firecrackers, bullets ricocheting, machinegun like rapid-fire, thunder in the sky in the middle of a rainstorm. There is lighting, there is smoke, great big thuds, crashing areal machinery past the burning body, fierce flashes in the sky, smell of acerbic electrical fire, splashes of falling and burning objects in my pond... all around me. My pond is not yet on fire. When a shot down drone falls, the second it hits the water the fire goes out immediately.

One of our octobots shoots out a stainless-steel wire entangling a dozen sets of propellers, an enemy robot limping on three motors, goes down and splashes into oily water. It splashes oily water on me. I have to close my mouth... I swallow oil... Loud whining noises, whooping sixobots fly overhead, along with quad robots with high-speed propellers. I can't see any lights... friendly drone?

Enemy taking on fire... crashing near the body. Not ours. Who is the enemy? I can see our octobot hovering in one place, sizing up the situation.

I bend forward and move my head out from under the ring. I want to twist off the ring, but it is better on. I'm sitting back in the water, but not before I take a good look around. Ahead of me the corpse's head is almost severed, or it is cut off half way attached by skin on the front of his body. My pond is bigger than I thought, extends about a hundred feet or more beyond my seat. I see other dead people in a straight line sitting on stones behind me... heads already submerged – three four heads? Some heads are higher than others, but not by much. The closest to me is fifteen feet. These folks had to have drowned already. These must have been the ones crying. Wonder why I'm alive? Wonder why I was brought here? Everyone behind me has drowned while I was sitting here. My seat was the highest of them all. Had I been the person behind me... I would already be dead.

I knew something was happening. When Olly put his hand on my shoulder and asked me if I felt something in my sphincter. I did. He must have slipped something under my skin. I'm glad he did. I had become a marked man. Like a cat, a dog, or an animal. Now I possess value!

I am guessing, but are they sending UA 60 Blackhawk choppers to get me or regular drones? We'll see. Terrible fight going on, mechanical screams all-over, ear-piercing squall, shrilling sounds mixing with heavy machinegun ratatata. It must be getting dark.

There has to be fifty or so flying machines – octobots, hexobots high pitched squeal, here comes a missile carrying ATGM. An (anti-tank guided missile). The coming tank must be autonomous. I hope there are no tanks involved, maybe there are special tanks out there. I can't tell, the noise is deafening.

The aerial clamor is continuous...

I hope my rescue robot is safe. Debris is falling around me; I need a metal umbrella. I am trying to straighten my metal cuff and putting it on the top of the ring. I can put only one cuff upon the ring the other cuff stays beside my ear because it won't go through the ring. I want to keep my head straight as I attempt to squat under the ring. The water would be almost at my mouth if I was sitting here. I'm safe from small debris. Now I can reach into my pockets – nothing in them. My little knife isn't there either, only wrinkled cloth and dirt.

What happened to my wallet, my little knife? I have underpants on, socks and the other shoe floated away. I'm feeling around … now I find my left shoe and the right one is up here on the cinder block. The shrieking noise is unbearable. Who is coming to rescue me and how?

WE ARE HIT! OUR MACHINE'S GOING DOWN! SENDING AN ARMOURED LAND ROVER, REMAIN WHERE YOU ARAE. I hear this command through the deafening noise. Was that message for me? I look at my screen… nothing but smoke. The message must have been for me. The air is full of different flying objects, X- wings, hover double X wings, some are crashing in my area.

I look up just in time to see a dark cloud approaching from the right. It is a cloud of ROACH-BUTS preparing to overwhelm my three blue light squad. Who is our commander? Olly? Klutch?

It is Klutch, I bet it is Klutch! I hear him yelling, no screaming; GET DOWN, CHARLES, DOWN, GET OUT OF THE WAY!!! ROACH BUTS EVERYWHERE!

I take a deep breath and go under the oily water. I start counting but can't hold my breath more than fifty count. I surface. The water is full of dying roach buts. Some still have enough battery power to move and stay on top of oil. Stainless steel wire everywhere stuck in propellers and hexbots – octobots, drones… screeching machines dropping from above, who can make any order out of this calamity?

I can see flashing lights to the left of the corpse. Could that be my rescue vehicle? Showing three blue lights … I'm safe!

More drones with three blue lights joining in the mix. They belch sticky substances over a large area, paralyzing high-speed propellers on enemy drones.

But now I still have to move away from this stone seat. I can still drown! My belt was attached to the flat bar behind me. A spring from a large wind-up clock? I can't take the belt with me I have to do all of this in oily water because it is up to my chest. My pants are falling down I have to keep them up by my hand. Now there is a BLACKHAWK drone splashing down right in front of me. My face is covered in oil. I have to breathe. Luckily, I can use my hands to wipe off the oil from my face. I spit out the oil and try not to swallow any. Maybe a little oil won't hurt me. But all the pollutants in it… could probably kill me. I taste acid, maybe lithium too, although I don't know what lithium taste like. Now that my belt is off, I attempt to wade through dead roach buts, out from the oily water, over to my Armored Rescue Vehicle ARV.

A hatch opens and a grinning face appears saying "good to meet you, Charles."

I ask; "you're Klutch?"

The world catches on fire behind me.

But I escape the fire.

*Hoffmann from the book "The Passengers" by Charles E. Jambor.

Manufactured by Amazon.ca
Bolton, ON

34532930R00085